Sunset Promises
A Second Chance Romance

by

Susan Mellon

Sunset Promises
A Second Chance Romance
Copyright 2022 by Susan Mellon

Editing: Precision Editing Group
Cover Design: Susan Mellon
Formatting: Susan Mellon
ISBN: 9798411201536

No part of this book may be reproduced, scanned, or distributed in any print or electronic form without written permission by Susan Mellon @ susanmellon.com. Please do not participate in or encourage piracy of copyrighted material in violation of the author's rights. Thank you for respecting the hard work of this author.

This is a work of fiction. Names, characters, places, and incidents are a product of the author's imagination. Locales and public names are sometimes used for atmospheric purposes. Any resemblance to actual people, living or dead, or to businesses, companies, events, institutions, or locales is completely coincidental.

Also Available by Susan Mellon

Not So Fake Series

Tag, You're It
Simon Says
Jacks

Sequels

The Locket
The Possibilities (Love Me in New York)

Standalones

The Fragrance of Love
Candlelight and Pancakes
Cuckoo for Love (A Quirky Love Story)
The Color of Music

Christmas

Christmas Anthology
~Three Separate Heartwarming Stories~

Join Susan's newsletter to get a free book.

It's Only Make-Believe (storyoriginapp.com)

Life is what happens while you're busy making other plans.

—John Lennon

Twenty Years Earlier

ONE

Tradd and Sunlyn arrived at Sunset Pier at the same time, each clutching a white envelope. The smell of saltwater wafted from the Atlantic Ocean into the warm evening breeze.

Sunlyn held her envelope up and grinned with excitement as Tradd greeted her with a peck on the lips.

"Let's sit on one of the benches farther on the pier," she suggested.

Tradd looked around. The pier was busier than normal tonight, with several people fishing and sightseeing. A seagull perched above one of the lights, hoping to catch scraps of food that might get dropped onto the pier.

"Sounds good to me."

She took his hand. The promise ring that Tradd had given her at junior prom, glittered in the sunlight.

They walked until they found a secluded bench and sat together. The hovering sun still shone brightly, not quite ready to slip behind the clouds and begin the evening's sunset.

"Are you nervous?" Tradd asked.

"No way. You?"

"Nervous . . . no. Excited . . . yes."

Laughter burst through Sunlyn's lips, floating above the sound of the surf from below. Sunlyn held up her hand for Tradd to see her index finger and thumb almost touching. "Okay, maybe a little."

"Let's do this on the count of three."

Sunlyn's shoulders heaved in anticipation. "One . . ."

"Two . . ." Tradd counted.

Just as Sunlyn was about to say "three," Tradd placed his hand over hers. "Wait!"

Sunlyn looked into his piercing eyes. "What?"

"No matter what happens. No matter what these letters say . . . either we both go to Vancouver Culinary, or no one goes."

"Oh, Tradd."

"Swear it." Tradd thrust his hand in the air with his pinky finger sticking out. "Pinky swear it, Sunlyn."

Sunlyn's hand went up, linking her small finger around his. "I pinky swear," she whispered, suddenly unsure whether that was a good idea or not.

Pinky swearing was their thing. They had started doing it a couple years ago over silly sophomore promises. This was different, though. This was real-life stuff. Serious stuff. These letters really mattered.

Tradd leaned in, kissing Sunlyn on her cheek, and whispered in her ear. "Three."

Cautiously, Sunlyn opened her envelope, being careful not to tear the letter inside, while Tradd tore his open like a child on Christmas morning.

"I got in!" they both yelled at the same time.

Sunlyn threw her arms around Tradd's neck. "I'm so happy."

"Me too!"

Sunlyn pulled back and reread her letter. "It says here that they're emailing a bunch of paperwork to read, print, and sign."

Tradd waved his hand through the air. "Cracker crumbs." His go-to saying for almost anything he considered incidental, yet important at the same time. In cooking, cracker crumbs served as the binding to hold ingredients together. One couldn't have one without the other. The same was true of the additional admission papers for the Vancouver Culinary Academy.

"I can't wait until Uncle Tom sees my acceptance letter," Sunlyn said.

"My mom is going to be over-the-moon ecstatic. What do you think about this name for our restaurant—"

"—What?" Sunlyn's brows shot upward. "You already have a name for it? We haven't even started classes."

"You know I'm a dreamer."

She elbowed him playfully. "I know. And that is so not my MO."

"So, do you want to hear it or not?"

"Of course I do."

"The Gathering Place." Tradd looked somewhere out in the distance, no doubt visualizing the sign of the restaurant.

"The Gathering Place." Sunlyn closed her eyes, thinking. "I like it."

"I just figured most people gather around tables during their meals. You know, making memories of being together and eating their favorite foods. Celebrating all the important milestones."

"Hey, you don't have to convince me. I like it, Tradd."

"Good. There's something I haven't told anyone . . . ever."

"Even me?"

"Yep." He gave her an impish grin.

"What is it?"

"I have a collection of recipes for our restaurant."

Something in Sunlyn's stomach turned sour. "Oh."

Tradd's smile disappeared. "What?"

Sunlyn's throat tightened. The last thing she wanted to do was burst his bubble. Tradd seemed to have everything planned, and they haven't even graduated yet.

They were supposed to leave for Canada the day after graduation. Why hadn't she pressed for a later start? And now he had a book of recipes that they were going to serve. Things were happening too fast. Didn't she have a say in the matter? They haven't even discussed what type of food they were going to offer, not to mention all the new things they would learn in school.

"It's just . . . we still have so much to learn." Sunlyn wrung her hands together. "And don't I get a say in what we get to serve?"

"That's a given, Sunlyn. However, I'm the chef. Your expertise lies with pastries."

"It's just, you seem to be in a big hurry to get to the rest of our lives. Is it so bad here?"

"I wouldn't use the word 'bad.' But there's a big world out there waiting for us. Don't you ever dream of our future together?" Tradd asked.

Sunlyn looked down at her promise ring. "Sure, I do. I mean—"

"—This is where you feel the closest to your parents," Tradd finished for Sunlyn.

"Kind of," Sunlyn murmured.

"Your parents will always be with you, no matter where you live."

"I know," Sunlyn agreed, standing. "You're right."

Tradd stood too. "Plus, we have each other. That makes everything else cracker crumbs."

"'Cracker crumbs,'" Sunlyn parroted, nodding.

"Let's go. I'll walk you home. You can call me later after you talk with your uncle." Tradd reached down, grasping Sunlyn's hand.

"For sure." But suddenly Sunlyn wasn't sure. About any of it.

Cracker crumbs, Sunlyn thought as they walked in silence toward the Beach Bum Beanery that her uncle owned. Tradd was so sure of how things were going to end.

She wished she was.

You're just being a nervous nellie, Sunlyn scolded herself as they walked. Everything was going to work out according to Tradd's dreams. Their dreams. After all, they were connected at the hip, weren't they? Everything else was just . . . cracker crumbs.

Convincing herself during the quick walk to her Uncle Tom's coffee shop, all Sunlyn had left to do was break the news to him. And that was something she wasn't looking forward to.

TWO

Glancing from his watch and then to the beanery door, for what seemed like the hundredth time, Tom grunted while pulling the trash bags from their receptacles. Emptying the trash was the last thing that needed doing after closing the shop for the day. A job he had given to Sunlyn two years ago. It was 8:00 p.m., time to close up shop for the day. And no Sunlyn.

Setting the heavy bag onto the floor with a thud, Tom winced, both hands landing on his lower back faster than an ice cube melting in the hot North Carolina sun. At the age of 63, his back creaked more than the hardwood floors of his beanery.

If it wasn't his back, it was his hips, and if it wasn't his hips, it was his knees protesting from the long hours. Waking at the crack of dawn almost every day to be at the coffee shop by 7:00 a.m. and staying until after the closing time of 8:00

p.m. Sometimes he wondered if he owned the shop or if the shop owned him?

Either way, it didn't matter. He loved owning the Beach Bum Beanery and living on the small island of Sunset Beach. Thirty-five years ago he had chosen the unbeaten path of easy-breezy days, staying out of the fast-paced corporate world and the big cities. Some called him a "beach bum," since he'd never settled down to make a family of his own.

But then again, families nowadays were different than the conventional families of the past. And he did have one. It had happened in an instant ten years ago. The date of May 24 would forever be engraved in his heart. Tom had become legal guardian of an eight-year-old at the age of 53, when most people were learning to navigate empty-nest syndrome.

He knew nothing about raising children. He would learn as he went. How hard could it be?

Shuffling to one of the coffee machines, Tom poured the last of the warm liquid into two paper cups and shuffled toward a table in the center of the small café. Sitting down, he sighed. He glanced around wearily. Soon he wouldn't be able to run his shop much longer, and it would be time to pass the torch to Sunlyn.

He had never broached the subject with her, but he was sure Sunlyn would be interested. When she wasn't looking, Tom kept a keen eye on her. She loved making the caffeinated beverages and mingling with the customers. Sunlyn even experimented with different flavors, making all the hip flavors that were popular with the younger crowd. She also had a flare for baking, making pastries to sell along with the coffee.

The door opened and Sunlyn slipped inside.

Fondness washed over Tom in a warm glow, knowing how much his brother and sister-in-law had missed out on watching her grow into a beautiful young lady.

Positive that Sunlyn was looking at him, he glanced at his watch once more to make his point. "You're late," he said, trying to sound perturbed. They both knew he wasn't. In fact, just the opposite. Sunlyn had him wrapped around her little finger. And she knew it.

"I'm sorry." She shrugged, noticing the garbage bags that were already sitting on the floor.

Tom waved his hand, dismissing her lateness. "You're here now."

"I have something to tell you," she said.

Tom chuckled. "Me too. You, first."

"No, no, Uncle Tom, you first."

"I insist. Beauty before age." He watched as Sunlyn's eyes sparkled. He liked that she lit up every time he said that, knowing full-well he deliberately flipped the saying that was probably old as the hills, or in their case, the ocean.

"I got accepted," Sunlyn said, sliding the white envelope across the table, then taking a sip of the coffee he'd made her.

A lump grew in his stomach. "Accepted to what?" He picked up the envelope reading the return address. *Vancouver Culinary.* "What's this about?"

"It's in Vancouver. In Canada."

"It always has been." Reaching up, he rubbed the whiskers protruding from his chin. A shave was in order.

"Right. It's from the college that I applied to."

Tom's eyes dropped back to the envelope and slowly met Sunlyn's. "I don't remember you mentioning that."

"I didn't," Sunlyn burst.

Those words took him by surprise. He'd thought they had an open-enough relationship to talk things through. Apparently not.

"I mean . . ." Sunlyn closed her eyes. "I wanted to be sure that I was accepted before I said anything. No use getting our hopes up. You know?" she asked, taking a long strand of her hair, twirling it in her fingers.

"And you didn't want my help with the papers? We haven't even toured the school—"

"—No, we didn't, but Tradd and his mom did—"

And there it was. "—Tradd Morrison?"

"That's right."

"I see."

"Uncle Tom, I'm sorry that I did this behind your back. I didn't want to worry you with all the details. You have your hands full with the beanery."

Tom rubbed his aching knees, leaning back in his chair. So, that was that. "And this is something you really want to do?"

"Uh-huh. Tradd and I have plans. We're going to open a restaurant one day. He'll be the chef, of course. And naturally, I'll be the pastry chef."

"Naturally." Would his brother approve? It wasn't like she was going to the local community college around the corner. She had chosen a school more than 3,000 miles away. In another country.

As if Sunlyn was trying to convince her uncle, she added. "It's a world-renowned school. One of the few in the world."

"Are you saying that for my benefit, or yours?"

"No one's, really. Just communicating."

Communicating? Is that what this was? "Congratulations, Sunlyn." He stood, taking a couple of steps toward his niece. She stood as well, hugging him. "When do classes start?"

"The day after graduation."

"That's in two weeks," Tom uttered, stepping back.

"I know it's sudden, but that's when Tradd wants to start."

Tom blinked at hearing Tradd's name, again. That's what this boiled down to. A boy. Who seemed to be calling all the shots. Did Sunlyn have any interest in going for herself?

"What did you want to talk to me about?" Sunlyn asked, trying to change the subject.

"To tell you the truth, I don't remember," Tom lied, walking around Sunlyn and grabbing one of the garbage bags.

Rushing toward him, Sunlyn grabbed the bag from his hand. "This is my job."

Tom forced a smile. "I got this. I need to get used to doing this again."

"Are you sure?"

"As sure as the tide rolls in and out."

Sunlyn released her hold on the bag. "Okay, then. I'll see you in a little bit. Thanks, Uncle Tom."

Tom watched as she walked back to the table and picked up her letter. Just as she headed toward the back door of the beanery, Tom called out to her. "Congratulations again, Sunlyn. I'm proud of you."

A smile greeted him just before she disappeared through the door.

And just like that, as fast as his family had come about, it was gone, for all intents and purposes.

Tom grabbed the two cups of coffee, tossing them into the trash bag. Dragging the bags outside to the garbage cans, he pulled the keys from his pocket and locked the coffee shop.

THREE

Standing in front of the open refrigerator door the following morning, trying to decide what to grab for a quick breakfast, Sunlyn heard muffled voices coming from the deck.

Who's talking?

She inched closer toward the glass door that was left ajar just enough for her to peer through while listening to the conversation.

Tom Bean and a woman sat at the round, turquoise-colored, umbrella-covered-table. The woman, dressed in business attire, slacks, and a blouse, was taking notes as her uncle talked.

"So, what's my next step?" Tom asked.

"If you want to move forward," the woman said, "I'll appraise the coffee shop." She took a sip of her coffee. "This is the height of the season to sell. This island will soon be buzzing with all the people staying on Sunset Beach."

"How soon can you post the for-sale sign? I want to take advantage of all the summer islanders."

"I can appraise it tomorrow. Once I do that, it'll take a day or two to review the numbers and meet with you again to discuss the asking price and go over everything with you."

"Great. The sooner the better," Tom said.

The woman closed her portfolio and leaned back in her chair. "I have to ask one more time. Are you sure you want to sell the Beach Bum Beanery?"

Sunlyn watched as her uncle looked toward the ocean. His beach house had the best view, and at night, once the island quieted, you could hear the surf. He nodded, as if he was communicating with the ocean tide. Then his gaze landed on the woman with short hair. His face schooled.

After a minute or two, he spoke. "It's not a question about me wanting to move forward. It's more about I don't have a choice."

Sunlyn's eyes narrowed. What was he talking about?

"I understand." The woman spoke softly. "It's not the easiest thing to accept when our children don't share the same dream. Are you sure she's not interested in taking over your shop?"

Tom's hand skated across his face. "I'm as sure as I can be without asking her. She has other plans."

Sunlyn's face heated from the realization of knowing they were talking about her.

The woman tapped her pen off the glass tabletop. "And you're sure you don't want to ask her?"

Ask me what? What's going on?

"I almost did yesterday, but . . ."

"But what?"

Tom sighed. "That's when she announced she was moving to Canada."

"Oh, I see."

"With a boy," Tom Bean continued. "Her high-school boyfriend made the plans for both of them, if you get my drift."

"Ahh . . . young love."

"That's not the half of it. Sunlyn and Tradd might think they're in love, but through these old eyes it's just a bad case of puppy love. Nothing more."

Sunlyn gasped, immediately slapping her hand over her mouth and hoping that her uncle hadn't heard. Watching as his head slowly turned in her direction, Sunlyn jumped back a few steps, scurrying into the kitchen.

Trying to look busy, Sunlyn began sifting through the ingredients in the coffee cupboard to see which items they had on hand.

"Shouldn't you be in school?"

Sunlyn jumped. Busted. Her eyes met her uncle's. His didn't look happy.

"Um . . ." She gulped. "Today is senior-skip day."

An honorary day that most seniors participated in before graduation. As an undergrad, Sunlyn had always thought it was a ridiculous idea. How could that even be an exciting day, knowing the higher-ups expected it. But now, Sunlyn decided to take advantage of the day. She'd earned it. Straight "A's". And to make the most of the day, Sunlyn was going to experiment with new coffee flavors.

"Don't most seniors hangout on the beach all day?"

"Some do. Others drive to Alligator Adventure in North Myrtle Beach," Sunlyn said.

"And yet you're home. Why?"

"I wanted to play around with a new coffee flavor and make chocolate-covered marshmallows for the coffee shop. Some of the regulars have been asking for them. I can always catch up with my friends later."

Although, she had no intention of doing that. She much preferred to stay away from large gatherings with classmates. During her school years, she'd mostly kept to herself making only a few close friends. The less she became attached, the better off Sunlyn knew she'd be.

Sunlyn watched as Tom glanced toward the deck. "Don't let me interrupt you and your friend," she said, stumbling over her words. "Er, coffee date, or meeting." Sunlyn motioned with her hand toward the deck. "Or whatever it is."

"It's business. That's all."

"I know."

Tom's eyes widened at her admission.

"I mean—"

"—No need to explain. I know you were listening." He turned on his heels and went back outside, closing the glass sliding door securely this time.

Sunlyn's mouth fell open, and her cheeks reddened.

She felt bad about him knowing she was listening to his conversation. Sunlyn didn't know why she did it. She'd just never seen her uncle have coffee with anyone at the house. Especially a woman. Sometimes he would have a buddy or two over to catch a game on TV, but that was the extent of it.

Chagrin washed through her, knowing there were more pressing matters that needed to be addressed other than listening to an uninvited conversation. Uncle Tom was planning on selling the beanery. He hadn't even asked her if she wanted it, to keep it in the family. She had thought he knew how much she enjoyed working there.

Apparently, he didn't.

And to top it off, what was with the "'puppy love'" comment? Her relationship with Tradd was more than puppy love. That she was sure of.

Sunlyn looked around the beach house that she had come to call home. It was decorated in shades of light gray, with blue and sand-colored hues to emulate the ocean and beach.

When she'd first arrived, as an eight-year-old, Sunlyn remembered thinking all the houses on Sunset Beach were weird, raised on stilts and with never-ending steps that led to multiple deck levels.

Then as she grew older, she learned coastal houses were built that way to protect them from the risk of hurricanes and strong storm surges. When she'd first arrived at the island, Sunlyn expected to find oars attached to the sides of the houses in case they were swept into the Atlantic during a storm.

Beach living was a far cry from growing up in Charlotte, NC. Her family had lived in a condo, and her father had worked inside a towering building for an architect firm while her mother worked at a bank. Boating and beaching were for vacations, not everyday living.

With each passing day, Sunlyn had learned to leave her past life behind, barely remembering what it was like, as she grew up on the small island, which was now her home.

Sadness crept through her veins. Her uncle had broken his promise to her last night when they'd talked, telling her he'd forgotten what he wanted to say. They'd promised each other a long time ago that they would be honest and upfront with each other. No secrets, his way of gaining Sunlyn's trust.

How could she leave knowing what she knew now?

"Canada," she muttered, hoisting herself onto the edge of the kitchen counter. "Oh, boy." Hadn't she done the same thing by not telling him about her school plans?

When did things change? The last thing she ever wanted to do was hurt her uncle. Slapping her hands off her thighs and jumping to the floor, Sunlyn grabbed the keys to her uncle's car.

A trip to Food Lion was in order. She would gather the items she needed to make his favorite dessert, and later the two of them would sit down and have a heart-to-heart talk.

FOUR

Pulling the fig cheesecake from the refrigerator after letting it cool for most of the day, Sunlyn set it gently on the kitchen island. Returning to the fridge, she pulled out the bowl of sliced figs for the garnish.

Sunlyn gently removed the cheesecake from the spring pan, placing it on a glass platter. Ignoring her phone that was buzzing in her back pocket, she began arranging the sliced figs on top of the cake.

She grabbed two plates from the cupboard and cut two slices of cheesecake. Stepping back to admire her creation, Sunlyn smiled.

"Perfect," she said, placing them on top of the container of chocolate-covered marshmallows for the beanery. It was almost 8:00 p.m.

Quickly swiping through the missed calls—that she had chosen to ignore—she left her phone on the counter. The last thing she wanted was to be interrupted by Tradd or her friends asking her where she was today.

Ten minutes later Sunlyn walked in the back door of the beanery and, as usual, her uncle was waiting for her with coffee at one of the tables. She set the plates of cheesecake on the table, along with two forks, and sat across from her uncle.

"What's this?" he asked.

"Your favorite," Sunlyn answered in a cheerful voice.

"I can see that. Why?"

"Because we need to talk."

"About what?" Tom asked, cutting into a bite with his fork.

"About the seagull in the room."

"The what?" her uncle asked right before eating his bite of cake.

"You know," Sunlyn giggled. "Like the elephant in the room. But I figured seagull was more appropriate, considering where we live."

He chuckled. "Go on."

"I'm sorry that I listened to your conversation this morning—"

"—Apology accepted."

"Is it true?" Sunlyn asked.

"You need to be more specific," her uncle said, setting his fork down and exchanging it for his mug of coffee.

"Do you really want to sell the Beach Bum Beanery?"

"I'm not getting any younger, Sunlyn."

Sunlyn watched as he continued eating his cheesecake. He was right. Tom Bean's hair was overrun with gray, and his face showcased lines. Although she hated to admit it, Sunlyn knew that these last few years her uncle had begun to slow down.

"But you're feeling okay, right? You're not selling because you're sick or something?" She didn't know where that had come from. She had never given it any thought before.

"No, no, nothing like that."

A sigh of relief escaped her lips. "If you need more help with your shop, I'm here."

Tom leaned back in his chair, pushing his empty plate aside. "For about another week, you are. Then what? You're headed to Canada."

"So," Sunlyn blurted.

"How would that work with you being more than 3,000 miles away?"

"Ask me to stay. I won't go."

Tom stood, shoving his hands into the front pockets of his blue jeans. "I won't do that, Sunlyn. This is my dream, not yours."

"I love working here!"

"Working here part-time is different than owning it. It's a 24/7 job."

"I know that. You sound like you don't want me here anymore." Where was all this coming from? Didn't he want her here? Had things changed that much?

"You need to create a life of your own. You started putting the wheels in motion with Tradd. Finish it."

"So that's what this is about. You're punishing me because of Tradd's plans." Sunlyn stood, meeting her uncle almost at eye level. "That's why you didn't tell me about your plan to sell. To punish me for not mentioning my plans for culinary school."

Tom shook his head. "Not true," he burst, then calmed his voice. "Everyone has to make their own path in life. Your parents did, I did, and now it's your turn. But make sure you are doing it for the right reason . . ."

"I don't understand. What do you mean?" Sunlyn asked, slumping into the chair again, confused.

"Through these eyes," Tom pointed to his face, "you're not making your plans. You're following Tradd's."

Sunlyn's brows knitted. Becoming perturbed with her uncle, she stood again. "Tradd and I are planning our future together. He loves me." Sunlyn snatched the container of chocolate marshmallows from the table and walked toward the display counter, setting them inside.

"How. How do you know? Has he ever told you that?" he pressed.

Sunlyn's face flushed as her ears stung from her uncle's question. Why was he doing this? Why was he being mean to her? Her uncle knew that she and Tradd were best friends from the first time they'd met five years ago. They were inseparable. They even shared the same dreams.

She opened her mouth to reply but closed it. That's when she noticed her uncle's eyes. His eyes weren't filled with meanness. The exact opposite. Uncle Tom's eyes shone bright with love for her. He wasn't there to hurt her.

Sunlyn couldn't bring herself to answer him. He was right. Tradd had never once said he loved her. What about the promise ring? Didn't that prove Tradd's love? Trepidation seeped through her as she looked at her uncle. He was waiting for her answer.

"I . . . I need to be by myself," Sunlyn vocalized, stepping from behind the counter and heading toward the door. "I need to think," she mumbled, looking back at her uncle once more, then slipped through.

The rolling tide lapped at Sunlyn's ankles as she walked barefoot along the edge of the beach. This wasn't how she'd envisioned the evening. Her uncle's question had pivoted their conversation in another direction. She needed to clear her head. Walking along the beach as the tide rolled back and forth was her happy place, where she went when she needed to think.

Does Tradd Morrison really love me? Sunlyn wondered. They were always together. Best friends since the first time they'd crashed into each other with their bikes. Sunlyn giggled at the memory.

She'd received a pink bicycle from her uncle, for her thirteenth birthday. Finally, she could galivant around the island by herself. Peddling as fast as she could, she'd veered to the right onto North Shore Drive, right in front of the Sunset Inn, at the exact time a boy was peddling just as fast as she was but coming from the opposite direction.

Before either knew what was happening, their bikes collided, the peddles latching, and they'd tumbled sideways, with Tradd on the bottom of the pile.

Andrea, the manager of Sunset Inn, had helped untangle them.

They'd been furious with each other. But Tradd had been the new boy at school that year, and he had singled Sunlyn out. Soon they were inseparable.

It was only natural that they'd started dating in high school. But were they high school sweethearts because they'd chosen it or just because it was almost expected of them, since they were always together anyway? It was easier.

Their relationship was comfortable and easy. Just like the trusted security blanket. Was that what they were?

Now Tradd had even planned the school they would attend together, the restaurant they would open together, right down to the name of the establishment, their responsibilities, and the menu. Tradd had even planned for them to be married when the time was right.

What if she wanted something different? A reasonable question, wasn't it?

FIVE

One week later a large sea of white-and-green graduation caps soared into the sky above the West Brunswick High School graduating class. Whoops and hollers could be heard across the football field from the students.

Needling his way through the mass of people, Tradd sought out Sunlyn. She had bent to pick up her cap. When she stood, her long, blonde hair shone in the sunlight, her graduation gown already draped over her arm.

"We did it!" Tradd shouted, pulling Sunlyn into his arms. The two of them laughed.

"Yes, we did. Finally!"

"Just think," Tradd said. "By this time tomorrow, we'll be in Canada."

Sunlyn nodded.

"Look, babe, I need to find my mom. A bunch of us are headed to Sunset Beach to hang out and celebrate. You're coming too, right? We'll be near the pier."

"I'm not sure—"

A knot formed in his stomach. "—Why not?" The last few days leading up to graduation Tradd had noticed a change in Sunlyn. He couldn't quite put his finger on what was bothering her. He'd hoped to pry it from her tonight.

"Uncle Tom said he wants to talk with me tonight."

"Can't it wait 'til later? Or tomorrow?"

Sunlyn shrugged. "I don't know. He sounded . . . kind of . . . sullen."

"Okay, sure," Tradd said, trying to shield his disappointment. He waved through the air above all the heads and shoulders of his classmates, trying to grab his mother's attention. "I think I see my mom. Just promise me you'll try to make it. Promise?"

Sunlyn sighed. "I guess I can try."

A wide smile appeared across his face. "I'll take it!" Pulling Sunlyn into his arms, he planted a quick kiss across her lips.

Joining her classmates a few hours later, Sunlyn's toes sank into the soft, billowy sand. Spotting the small group of classmates she'd spent the last ten years with, Sunlyn opted to head a little closer to the surf.

Plopping down on the wet, flat sand, Sunlyn looked around for sandpipers. She preferred their company. They were amusing surfbirds, always on the move, running back and forth. This evening three of them foraged for an evening snack in the sand near her.

"Hello, Larry, Mo, and Curly." Sunlyn laughed at the names she had given to the sandpipers. The Three Stooges. Her dad's favorite.

Sunlyn had never warmed up to their slapstick humor, but after coming to live with her uncle, it brought her comfort. Oh, sure she knew these particular sandpipers weren't the same ones that she'd named ten years ago, but she couldn't bring herself to change their names.

Her eyes glazed at the incoming tide, watching it roll in and out. In a weird kind of way, Sunlyn thought it was bringing a piece of her parents back to her.

"Babe, you made it," Tradd called out, interrupting her thoughts, sitting next to her.

Sunlyn looked over at Tradd. How lucky was she to have such a cute boyfriend? He had brown curly hair and the biggest dimples she'd ever seen.

"Yep." She redirected her gaze to the never-ending ocean view.

"What are you thinking about?"

"The ocean. Isn't it beautiful?"

"Sure. I guess." Tradd shrugged. "I'd rather think about Canada."

Sunlyn cocked her head at Tradd. He was always thinking forward. Never appreciating the moment he was in. Restless. Uncontented.

"But the ocean is here now . . . right in front of us."

"I know. I see it every day."

"So do I." Sunlyn bumped shoulders with Tradd. "But it's vastness is amazing. The flow of the ocean. I mean, the Atlantic touches other countries like Bermuda and even as far away as Russia." Sunlyn leaned forward and cupped a handful of the saltwater. "And we can't see those places from here, but this water has touched their shores. Don't you find that interesting? This really is a small world we live in." Sunlyn let the water cupped in her hand fall onto Tradd's legs.

"Hey, you." Tradd laughed.

"I'm thinking too heavy again, aren't I?" Sunlyn asked. Not that it really mattered. It didn't. Her parents were out there somewhere. It was an automatic response when she wanted to feel closer to them.

"Just a pinch." He winced for effect.

"Listen, I need to tell you something." Sunlyn turned to face him.

"You're breaking up with me, aren't you?"

"What? No." Sunlyn playfully hit Tradd's arm. "Why would you even ask that?" Sunlyn watched as his Adam's apple bobbed.

"It's just, well, you've been acting weird all week. You know, like you want to tell me something, but then you don't."

"Um. I do. I'm not flying to Canada with you. I switched my flight." Her brows arched at the same time her shoulders scrunched upward, not quite knowing what to expect from him.

His face schooled as he jumped up. Sunlyn jumped up with him.

Why doesn't he say something? Is he upset? Angry? Disappointed?

"Why?"

"Uncle Tom needs my help with the beanery." *He just doesn't know it yet.*

"Can't someone else help? That's pretty selfish of him to expect you to change your plans so suddenly."

Sunlyn shook her head adamantly. "That's selfish on your part, Tradd Morrison! Where would I be if my uncle hadn't taken me in after my parents died? I owe him."

"You owe him?"

"It's just for a day or so." Sunlyn crossed her fingers behind her back. *Was it?*

Tradd folded his arms across his chest. "Fine."

"Fine, what?"

"I'll change my flight too. What's your flight number?" He pulled his cell phone from his pocket, opening the airline's app.

"No. Don't." Sunlyn sighed loudly. "You go on ahead of me."

"You'll be traveling alone. I don't like that idea."

Sunlyn stomped her foot in the sand. "You don't have a say in the matter, Tradd. Besides, your classes start the next day."

"And so do yours."

Sunlyn softened her stance. "Listen, this is our last evening together on the island. Are we seriously going to argue over this? I told you we should've waited until fall to start the culinary curriculum, but you insisted on us starting now."

"How long have you known?"

"What does that matter?"

"How long? You've been walking around here brooding about this. If you had told me sooner, I could've changed my flight too. How long have you known, Sunlyn?"

"About a week."

"Wow. What does that even mean?"

"It means that I made up my mind a week ago to postpone my flight. But my uncle just found out a little while ago."

"Wow!"

"Come on, Tradd. This is our last evening together. Can we just enjoy it?" Sunlyn peered at the sky. Shades of pink began replacing the blue. "We still have a little bit of time before the sun sets. Let's not fight."

"You're right. Let's walk the beach."

"Let's walk to the Kindred Spirit Mailbox and write something in the journals."

"I don't know."

"Please, please, please," Sunlyn insisted, standing on the tips of her toes and kissing Tradd on his cheek. Sunlyn watched as a tiny smile broke the barrier of his face. She'd succeeded.

His head motioned in the direction of the mailbox. "We should hurry if we're going to make it before it gets completely dark out here."

Clapping her hands, Sunlyn headed in the direction of the mailbox and hollered over her shoulder. "Come on slow-poke!" She waited for him to match her stride and then reached down, linking her fingers through his.

She knew she had hurt Tradd's feelings. But what could she do? If she had told him sooner, Tradd would have changed his plans. That was the last thing she wanted.

For the last four years all Sunlyn heard was Tradd talking about this world-renowned school for cooking. There was no way she wanted to hinder his plans.

Tradd was a dreamer. He had wanderlust.

Sunlyn was cautious and didn't like change.

Was that the same thing as oil and water?

"Earth to Sunlyn . . . did you hear me?" Tradd asked, interrupting her musings.

"I'm sorry. What did you say?"

"How about I play our song while we walk." Tradd was already sifting through his phone's playlist.

"I'd love it."

A few seconds later "We Have All The Time In The World," by Louis Armstrong, rang out while Sunlyn and Tradd walked in silence.

Present Day

SIX

The hum of chatter filled The Gathering Place in Manhattan, New York. Tradd Morrison smiled as he walked through his restaurant. This was the fruit of a lifetime of dreaming and decades of work.

The first few years in Vancouver, where he had graduated at the top of his class. Six more years in Europe, where he had studied under the direction of world-famous chefs. Then the last ten years in New York, where he had opened The Gathering Place.

Focusing on fine dining, Tradd had managed to win over the elites of the city. The restaurant opened at 4:00 p.m., and closed when the clock struck midnight. Reservations only. And within the last couple of years, he had seen the waiting list stretch three months out.

Carrying a case of champagne to the bar area, Tradd now smiled, greeting customers that were enjoying a drink while waiting for their tables. Setting the case on the floor behind the bar, Tradd waited for his head bartender, Mitch, to finish mixing what looked like, to Tradd, a cosmopolitan.

Mitch strolled over to Tradd. "Hi, Boss," he said, smiling.

"Mitch." Tradd squeezed his shoulder. "What time does your assistant arrive?" Tradd glanced at his watch. It was 8:00 p.m., and Tradd still had items to discuss with Mitch before he left for North Carolina.

In ten years, this was only the second time Tradd had left the restaurant, handing over the reins both times to Mitch. The Gathering Place was Tradd's baby, requiring a 24/7 commitment.

The first time Tradd had left, the trip had lasted only three days. For the death of his mother. His mother kept her arrangements simple: she wished to be cremated, with no service, and for her ashes to be scattered in the Atlantic. This trip, however, would be a little longer. Tradd needed to clean out her beach house and list it for sale.

A small group of women had just entered The Gathering Place. They laughed together as the hostess led them to their table in the middle of the restaurant.

"She'll be in around 9:00 p.m.," Mitch answered.

Cranking his neck, Tradd watched as the woman with long, blonde hair turned toward one of the other women she was with and stuck her tongue out at her. A warm feeling of *déjà vu* washed through him. *Is that...* Tradd wondered.

"Hey, Tradd! Earth to Tradd, are you listening?" Mitch asked his boss, lightly hitting his palm off the top of the bar, trying to capture his attention.

"What?" Tradd looked at Mitch. "Yeah, whatever, fine," he said, heading in the direction of the women.

Tradd's eyes zeroed in on the small group—a brunette, a fiery red-head, a silver-haired, and one beautiful blonde. He was sure he knew the blonde. She was of average height and slim.

Making his way closer to their table, Tradd didn't see the server headed toward him. She was carrying a large, oval platter filled with several beverage glasses. In an instant, his elbow bumped into the tray, throwing the server off balance. The glasses crashed to the floor, turning the heads of anyone within earshot.

"Hey!" the young server hollered, holding the empty tray in her hand.

"Ah, man!" Tradd's eyes focused on the mess. Holding both his hands up, he first assured the diners that everything was okay, then turned his attention toward the server. "I'm sorry. I'll get someone to clean this." The server's face was a shade of crimson. "Whoever those drinks belonged to, please let them know they'll get dessert on the house for the delay. Excuse me."

After sending another employee to clean the mess, he headed straight to the women's table. There she was. Could it really be Sunlyn, after all these years? What was she doing here? Did she decide to look for him? There was no way this was a coincidence.

Two more steps, and Tradd was at her side. Reaching forward, he lightly touched her shoulder. "Sunlyn?"

The woman turned in her chair to face him. "Excuse me?"

Tradd's hand dropped to his side. It wasn't Sunlyn. "I'm . . . sorry . . . I thought you were someone else."

The blonde-haired woman smiled. "No worries," she muttered, returning her attention back to the women.

Dunderhead! he mentally kicked himself, rushing to the sanctuary of his office.

Leaning back in his chair, Tradd's fingers threaded through his hair. How could he make such a mistake like that? He hadn't thought of his high-school sweetheart in years. Perhaps it was the stress of going back to Sunset Beach.

A knock on his office door drew his attention back to the present. "Hey, Mitch, come in."

Tradd had hired Mitch almost right out of the gate. Mitch was great at interacting with the customers and had a drop-dead smile that encouraged the ladies to linger around the bar just a little longer to enjoy another drink. He had good business sense, too, which Tradd valued most when he had to make infrequent trips like this.

"What was that?" Mitch asked, exaggerating his speech. He sat across from Tradd, linking his fingers behind his bald head.

"A ghost."

"A what?"

Half sighing and half grunting, Tradd shook his head. "It was nothing. I thought I saw someone I once knew."

"Oh, I get it." Mitch smiled. "A past relationship coming back to haunt you, eh?"

"Something like that. Anyway, my flight leaves tomorrow morning. Do you have the order ready for what you need at the bar? I already put the order in for the kitchen."

"Check your email."

"I'll do that. The schedule is finished for the next two weeks. You just need to print and post it. I'll email it to you later tonight."

"Will do."

"I shouldn't be gone more than a week."

"If you say so." Mitch shrugged.

"What's that supposed to mean?" After the incident in the dining room, he wasn't sure if he felt more perturbed at Mitch's carefree manner or at himself for even thinking that woman was Sunlyn.

"From where I sit, it's going to take longer than you think. I mean, your mom's house has been boarded up for, what . . . a year now?"

"Yep."

"Trust me. Been there, done that. It takes longer than a week to clear out a lifetime of stuff."

Tradd clenched his fists on his lap. He hated to admit it, but his friend was probably right. "Not if I can help it. I'll have my cell on me 24/7 if you need me."

"Sure thing, boss. I'm wondering, though."

"What's that?" Tradd asked, sifting through a stack of papers on his desk, trying not to think about Sunlyn and hoping Mitch would take the hint that he was busy and go back onto the floor.

"Who is she? I don't remember any woman getting you flustered like this."

Tradd blew out a puff of hot air. She was the last one he wanted to talk about. "We were together in high school."

"From your reaction, I'd say she was more than a high-school fling."

"I thought so, too."

"How come I never heard this before?" Mitch asked.

"I like to look forward, not backward."

"Out with it. What's the deal with her?"

"I'll give you the abridged version. We met at the ripe old age of thirteen, started dating at sixteen, and apparently broke up after graduation. The end."

"Seriously, boss?"

"Sometimes it's best to let sleeping dogs lie, know what I mean?"

"If you say so."

"Listen, I still have to put payroll into the computer."

Mitch stood. "I can take a hint. Good luck with your mom's house, and have a safe flight."

Finally, Tradd was alone. Now maybe he could finish his work. After the restaurant closed later this evening, he still had to finish packing. Quickly processing the payroll, he tried not to think about the blonde woman he'd mistaken for Sunlyn.

Twenty years had passed since he'd last seen her. Why would he think she'd suddenly appear in Manhattan? He hadn't even seen her after his mother died. For all Tradd knew, she wasn't living on the small island any longer.

Twenty years was a long time. She could be anywhere. Did she ever go away to school? Maybe she owned her own bakery or worked as a pastry chef. Knowing Sunlyn, she was probably married with a couple of kids in tow. All questions he wondered about. Answers he knew were none of his business now.

SEVEN

After closing and locking the backdoor to the Beach Bum Beanery, Sunlyn skirted across the street to her home. Entering her kitchen, she poured herself a glass of white zinfandel. Then stepping from her flip-flops, Sunlyn began the climb to the top deck of her modest beach house.

Settling into one of the two Adirondack chairs, Sunlyn set her glass on the deck next to her chair. Then she hugged her knees to her chest and took a long swallow of wine.

Giggling as her free hand threaded through her golden-yellow strands, she remembered what the decks were called. Even after all these years, Sunlyn still giggled about the term "poop decks."

Remembering when she had first arrived at Sunset Beach thirty years ago, she sighed. Uncle Tom had taught her the name of the decks. And for the longest time she'd thought he was teasing.

Growing up, Sunlyn had learned that the "strange name" originated from the French word for "stern." The "poop deck" provided elevated positions ideal for observation, one of Sunlyn's favorite ways to unwind after a long day of work at the small coffee shop she owned.

And today was one of those days.

Sitting high atop the small barrier island, Sunlyn enjoyed watching the ocean tide roll in and out, caught up in the brightness from the shining moon.

Just like the tide, her regular customers had rolled in and out today. All with the same name rolling off their lips: Tradd Morrison.

Tradd back at Sunset Beach. Was it true? Perhaps it was all just rumors. But Sunlyn knew better. Too many people were talking about him for it not to be true.

Truth be told, it was expected. Sunlyn just hadn't known when.

About a year ago, she had heard his mother had passed away in a nursing home in Calabash. No viewing. No funeral. Now he was back. Probably to sell the house on Sunset Beach. It wasn't as if he needed it. Her regular customers had told Sunlyn he lived in New York.

The house had been boarded up since Tradd's mother had moved into the nursing home. Or so Sunlyn had heard. Still, after all these years, she stayed away from North Shore Drive. Which wasn't an easy thing to do, considering that one had to pass right by the street to leave the island.

She never turned to look while driving, keeping her eyes focused forward as if she had blinders on.

Too many memories.

It was as if she had been walking on eggshells since his mother's death. Every time the small bell that hung above the door of the Beach Bum Beanery rang out, announcing another customer, Sunlyn held her breath.

Now he was back, and it was only a matter of time before she and Tradd would run into each other. Or, worse yet, Tradd would stop in the beanery for a coffee.

Pulling her phone from the back pocket of her peach-colored capris, Sunlyn opened her text notifications. She scanned to the bottom of her messages, where Tradd Morrison's texts were safely tucked away from view. From twenty years ago.

How pathetic, Sunlyn thought. Who did that? Who saved messages for that long? Especially from someone who had moved on without her.

Her slender finger hovered over his name. Should she, or shouldn't she? She shrugged, lightly tapping his name. The last time she had read these was when Sunlyn had heard Tradd's mother passed.

Taking another swallow of wine, she scanned the messages.

On and on the messages continued. The first few days after he had left for Vancouver there were several, along with phone calls. All went unanswered. Then little by little the messages slowed until they finally stopped altogether. And that was when she had stopped wearing her promise ring.

She'd let him believe that she was scheduled to arrive in Canada a few days after his arrival. But she'd never booked the flight. And how could she explain that to him? Silence had been easier.

Sunlyn couldn't blame Tradd for giving up on her.

Sunlyn rushed into the coffee shop the following morning, hands full of chocolates to sell. Mary, her best friend and hired help, was pouring coffee for customers.

"Thanks for covering for me," Sunlyn said, kneeling behind the counter to stash half the chocolate-covered marshmallows and homemade peanut butter cups in the display case. She stowed the other half in the small refrigerator to keep the chocolates cold.

Mary looked at Sunlyn. "You do know that's going to cost you additional chocolates," she teased.

Laughing, Sunlyn held up a small container with Mary's name written across the lid in black marker. "Got you covered."

The bell on the door jangled, causing Sunlyn to stand up to greet the customer, an automatic response after twenty-plus years behind the counter.

Her eyes met Tradd's.

Time froze. At least to Sunlyn. In what seemed like several minutes of awkwardness, which was probably only a few seconds in real time, Sunlyn ducked behind the counter, closing her eyes.

No, no, no! Not already. I look like an urchin.

Mary cleared her throat, looking from Sunlyn to Tradd, and back to Sunlyn again. "You do know he saw you, right?" Her hand rested on her hip.

"Shush!" Sunlyn held her finger to her mouth.

"She's right, you know," Tradd injected.

Embarrassed, Sunlyn stood. Where was a conch shell when she needed one? She wished she could crawl inside the seashell. She could just imagine what she looked like to him, in her old pair of leggings and chocolate-stained T-shirt. Sunlyn's hand reached up to tame the strands of hair that had escaped her messy bun.

Of all the times to dress like a scoundrel. Tradd couldn't have picked a worse day. What was he doing here, anyway? She closed her eyes. Her customers had warned her that Tradd was back at Sunset Beach.

Tradd had on a simple pair of cargo shorts and a button-down shirt, cuffs rolled to his elbows. He looked the same. No signs of aging, unless you counted the few strands of silver that edged his temples.

"Tradd . . ." What else could she say? Should she say? Twenty years was a long time.

"Sunlyn, you look . . ." Sunlyn watched as his eyes roamed from the top of her messy bun to the tips of her painted, bright-green toes protruding from her flip-flops. His head tilted. "Busy."

Busy? Tradd hasn't seen her in twenty years and that's the best he could say?

She ran her hand behind her neck and remembered she'd forgone makeup today, as well. *Oh boy!* Maybe busy wasn't that bad, after all. At least it was polite.

"I am," Sunlyn said, grabbing her work apron from the hook and slipping it over her head. She couldn't do anything about the no-makeup thing, but she could hide the smeared chocolate across her T-shirt.

"I just came by for a couple of coffees. Regular. No cream or sugar."

Not one, but two. Was he with someone? A quick glance around told her he wasn't. Maybe the other recipient was waiting in the car or at his mom's beach house.

"Sure, let me get that for you." Sunlyn moved toward the coffee machine, rolling her eyes at Mary. She knew Mary was working the counter this morning, but she needed to do something with her hands. Blowing out a puff of hot air, she calmed a bit.

After pouring the coffees, she handed them to Tradd.

"How much do I owe you?" he asked.

Sunlyn shook her head. "It's on the house."

"I can't let you do that."

"I insist."

"Fine." Reaching in his pocket, Tradd pulled out some one-dollar bills, depositing them into the glass "Tips" jar sitting next to the cash register. "Maybe I'll see you around."

Sunlyn's eyes widened. "Maybe."

Tradd walked out of her shop as fast as he walked in.

She let out a long, loud breath, then turned, pounding her head off the light-brown wall. "He tipped me! Tradd Morrison had the nerve to tip me!"

"Easy, now," Mary said, stepping closer and wrapping her arm around Sunlyn's shoulders. "Better pace yourself. There's no telling how long he'll be on the island."

Sunlyn gave the wall a break. "And that's supposed to make me feel better?" Her brow raised.

Mary shrugged. "I don't want to see you end up with a concussion."

Sunlyn grabbed the tip jar, pulling out the bills he'd placed inside. "Three dollars!"

"That's pretty generous, just for coffee, don't you think?"

"Generous? More like insulting. I told him the coffee was on the house, and then what does he do? He drops a tip in the jar worth more than the coffee. Really?"

"Just saying." Mary grabbed a rag, wetting it under the spigot, and began wiping off the tables.

Sunlyn shoved the bills back into the jar.

Reaching into the display case, she grabbed two peanut butter cups. Chocolate would help. She peeled the paper from the treat, popping one into her mouth. Of course, a hot shower, clean clothes, and makeup would help too.

EIGHT

Tradd tossed his keys onto the kitchen island in his mother's beach house and set both coffees down. He was unsure of how he felt about seeing Sunlyn again. By her reaction, Sunlyn was unnerved at seeing him again too. A smile turned up the corners of his mouth as he reached for one of the coffees.

Hmm, not bad, he thought after taking a sip. He relished a good cup of coffee. Sunlyn's coffee could almost give the Plaza a run for its money. Almost. The Plaza ranked as the best coffee he'd ever tasted, and he was lucky enough to live in the same wonderful city.

It felt surreal to be back at the beach house he had called home. It felt dark and lonely. Not so much from the lack of anyone living inside, but from the lack of natural light.

Toward the end, before she'd ended up in a nursing home, his mother had begun to get paranoid and kept the blinds closed and the curtains drawn.

The first job was to take down those awful drapes. Window by window, he went through the whole house, removing the curtains. Some were even covered in cobwebs on the underside from not being opened in years. After he dusted and opened the blinds, sunlight flooded into the home he remembered as a boy.

Gravitating back to the other cup of coffee, his mind wound its way back to Sunlyn. It was almost too hard to believe that she'd never left the small North Carolina Island. He'd never expected to still see her at the Beach Bum Beanery. What had happened to her dreams of becoming a pastry chef? Did her uncle have that much of a hold over her?

Remembering the way her blonde hair was piled on top of her head this morning, Tradd chuckled. She looked pretty much as he remembered. Still thin, with green eyes that sparkled like . . . mint tourmalines. She was too special to have eyes that sparkled like ordinary green emeralds—at least, in his mind.

Tradd had spent some time emptying all the kitchen cabinets. Then grabbing the last of his coffee, he went outside and sat on the deck. He pulled his phone from the pocket of his shorts and checked the time. Noon. What had happened to the morning? His stomach rumbled as if on cue. To get started on the house Tradd had decided to skip breakfast. Not his best idea.

Sifting through his contacts, Tradd pressed the icon next to Mitch's name. The phone rang several times before landing in voicemail. "Hey, this is Mitch. Leave me a message, and when I have some time, I'll call you back." A loud beep resonated in Tradd's ear.

"Hey, Mitch. It's Tradd. Call me back and let me know how things are going at the restaurant." Leaning back in his chair, Tradd ended the call. His eyes closed as he listened to the sounds of the birds in the marsh.

Growing up, Tradd had loved that the back of his house faced the saltmarsh. At one time, he could name the different birds just by their unique sounds. Especially in the evenings, as the sun was setting and the birds began to settle in for the night.

Nowadays, he wouldn't be able to do that. But, living in New York City, he could name every delivery truck just by the sound of its engine idling outside his restaurant. That had to account for something, right?

The persistent ringing stirred Tradd from his sleep. He didn't remember any birds sounding like that. Then his eyes flew open.

"Mitch," Tradd uttered into the phone after answering it.

"Boss. What's up? How's the house coming?"

"I. Um . . ." Tradd took a few seconds to get his bearings. "Man, I fell asleep. What time is it?"

Mitch roared with laughter. "Dude, it's 5 o'clock. I figured I'd call you back before we get too busy in here."

"Wow. A few minutes ago, it was noon." Tradd stood and stretched.

"More like several hours ago. You're supposed to be clearing the house out, not sleeping your days away."

"Yeah, yeah. I know."

"I mean, I've never known you to sleep in the day," Mitch said.

"I don't—"

"—Until now."

Tradd watched as two great egrets flew together, landing in the marsh. Tradd smiled; he'd never seen that in the city. Just pigeons. "Sleepless night. Early flight. Anyway, how's it going?"

"Great."

"'Great,'" Tradd mimicked.

"Boss, you just left yesterday. What did you think I'd say? I mean, you put me in charge of running this place for a reason. Either you trust me, or you don't."

"Come on, Mitch, don't spin it like that," Tradd barbed.

"Just saying. I'd ask how the house was coming along, but given the fact that you slept the day away, I'd say it's not."

Reaching up, Tradd rubbed the back of his neck. His friend had a point. "I'm hanging up now. What does that tell you?"

Mitch chuckled. "What does this tell you? Don't call me. I'll call you."

Tradd swiped the icon ending the conversation, roaring with laughter. He knew his restaurant was in good hands with Mitch—he just needed to be reminded. Tradd wasn't used to being away from The Gathering Place.

Sitting in his Avis rent-a-car on the corner of North Shore Drive and Sunset Blvd., Tradd had a decision to make. Turn right and head toward Calabash, or make the left and head toward the Beach Bum Beanery. The coffee shop stayed open well into the evening.

Glancing at the car's clock, he noticed it was already 6:30 p.m. He made the left. Although Tradd didn't remember the shop serving sandwiches, he'd take whatever she sold and then head back to the house to get some more work done.

Two minutes later he walked into the coffee shop. Most of the tables were empty, apart from an elderly couple sitting in the middle, holding hands and drinking coffee. Pausing, he wondered if one day that would be him. Except he more envisioned the Plaza.

Standing at the counter, Tradd eyed the small selection of pastries. There were a few muffins, a variety of cookies, two different pies, and a mixture of chocolates. *Welcome to small-town living,* he thought.

"Tradd." A woman's voice rang out, grabbing his attention.

He looked up. "Hi, Sunlyn." Inwardly he chuckled, noticing that she'd changed from her morning's attire. She had on a pair of turquoise-colored capris with a soft pink, sleeveless top. Her hair had changed as well, secured tightly into a ponytail. A touch of makeup and lip gloss dusted Sunlyn's already sun-kissed complexion.

"What are you doing here?"

Is that how she greets all her customers? "Thought I'd grab another cup of your coffee and a bite for dinner."

"Oh. Well. The Beach Bum Beanery doesn't have a dinner menu." She shrugged. "Or a lunch menu," she added for good measure.

"No worries. I'm not overly hungry," Tradd lied. "I'll have two muffins and a small bag of chocolates to take back to the house. Oh, and a cup of coffee . . . for here."

"Not much of a dinner, if you ask me. Have a seat. I'll bring it to you," Sunlyn said in an urbane manner.

Tradd sat at one of the tables near the window, sighing. He couldn't figure out if Sunlyn was annoyed with him being there or if this was her new normal. A person sure could change in twenty years.

Sunlyn set a bag with his order in front of him, along with a cup of coffee, and napkins. "Let me know if you need anything else. I close at 8:00

p.m." She tore a small, green receipt from her pad and laid it on the table.

"Will do." *Well, that much hasn't changed.* Tradd hurriedly reached out, grabbing Sunlyn's hand to stop her. A charge shot through him. Sunlyn stopped and looked at him. *Think, man. Say something.* "Still closing up shop the same time, I see."

"More or less. If I sell all the coffee, I close earlier."

"Speaking of, what's in this cup of joe?" Tradd motioned toward his mug.

"Trade secret. Sorry." Her lips quirked.

"Care to join me?" he asked impulsively.

"I don't know," she murmured.

He watched as Sunlyn glanced around the shop.

"Come on, for old-time's sake. A minute or two won't hurt."

He watched as Sunlyn cautiously sat in the empty chair across from him. Did she look nervous? What was there to be nervous about? They were just chatting for a few minutes. Unless. His eyes dropped to her hands. Was she married? Skimming over her fingers for a ring, he sighed. Her fingers were bare.

"I guess," Sunlyn agreed.

"How have you been? It's been a while."

"Good. You?"

"Fine. Busy."

"Great. Me too." Sunlyn swallowed. "How is it living in New York?"

Tradd's head tipped in her direction. How did she know that was where he lived? Was she checking up on him? If she knew, why hadn't she tried reaching out?

"Fine. Have you been checking up on me?" he teased with an impish grin.

Sunlyn's head cocked, and her cheeks warmed. "No," she said adamantly. "The customers mentioned it recently."

"I see," Tradd muttered through a sip of coffee, not sure if he believed her. "How's Sunset Beach?"

"Still here." Sunlyn stood. "I'd better get back to work."

"Oh sure, I need to get back to the house. It was nice running into you again." Tradd stood, dropping a ten-dollar bill on the table to cover his coffee and baked goods.

"I guess . . . but we didn't exactly run into each other. You came into my coffee shop."

He shook his head. Always cagey. "So I did. Maybe I'll see you around."

"Maybe," Sunlyn said, scooping the money and check off the table.

Tradd snatched up his order and left. What was with them? That conversation had been horrible. Had they changed that much over the years?

Conversation had always flowed easily between them. They were high-school sweethearts, for crying out loud. Or, at least, they used to be. Surely there was some thread of evidence still hanging around of that. Or why did he go into that crazy zone the other day at his restaurant when he thought she'd showed up out of the blue?

One thing hadn't changed. Sunlyn was still the same heedful girl he remembered.

NINE

The following morning, before the heat of the day settled in, Tradd headed to the beach for an early morning walk, part of his normal routine back in New York—walking to work every day.

Kicking off his loafers and setting them next to the entrance of the beach, Tradd stepped into the sand, wiggling his toes in the loose grains. The beach was almost deserted. There were a few people with buckets digging for shells, along with a few fishermen trying their luck in the waves.

Trodding in the soft sand was more of a workout than he remembered. It definitely didn't compare to walking the flat sidewalks in Manhattan. As he walked, the white sand reflected the morning's sun and had Tradd wishing he hadn't forgotten to pack his sunglasses. Making a mental note to purchase a pair when he went for a paint run later that morning, he continued to walk along the beach.

He stopped to admire the ocean tide rolling in and listened to the sound. In the next beat, he felt something crawling across his foot in the sand. He jumped back a step or two. Losing his footing in the uneven sand, he stumbled, falling onto his butt.

"Whoa," he muttered, laughing.

"What's the matter? Afraid of a little sand-crab?"

Tradd's head spun around to see Sunlyn standing a few feet away in the water's edge. Jumping up and brushing the sand from his shorts, he joined her in the surf.

"You saw that, huh?"

Sunlyn nodded.

"Hey, a guy can't be too careful. If this was New York, that probably would have been a spider or a rat running across my foot."

"But this isn't New York—"

"—And I wouldn't be walking around the streets in my bare feet."

Sunlyn softly giggled. "Good point."

Tradd's eyes glistened, listening to her laughter. That was the Sunlyn he remembered. The beach was her happy place, where she felt carefree and most comfortable. A warm glow poured through him, realizing that he missed her laughter.

At a loss for words, Tradd rattled off the first thing that came to mind. "So, do you come here often?" *That was stupid.*

Sunlyn's brows raised. "Does that line work with the ladies back in the Apple?"

"Just making conversation."

"Well . . . in that case. Yes, I do come here almost every day while my muffins and pies cool."

Cupping his watch with his hand, he read the time and whistled. "It's 7:30. You must get up awfully early to bake."

"Usually."

The waves nipped and teased their ankles as the tide rocked back and forth while a sandpiper ran along the beach ahead of them.

"How have you been?" Tradd asked. He missed her and the life they had planned together.

"The shop is busy. Business is good."

"No. Not the beanery. You. How are you?" Tradd asked again.

"Oh. I'm . . ." Sunlyn swallowed hard. "I'm good."

"I remember my mom telling me that Tom had passed away."

Sunlyn nodded, splashing the saltwater with her foot.

"And you still stayed in Sunset Beach?"

Jerking her head in Tradd's direction, Sunlyn slid her sunglasses on top of her head. "Of course. Why wouldn't I?"

"I don't know?" Tradd shrugged. "Thought maybe you would have looked me up or something."

"Seriously?"

"Sure, why not? I mean, we made plans for our future together. Remember?"

A gasp escaped Sunlyn's lips. She pushed her sunglasses back onto the bridge of her nose. "I should head back. I'm sure my pies have cooled by now."

In the next instant, she was walking away so fast that she looked like she couldn't wait to get away from him.

What was all that about?

Just when the conversation was easing, it tightened back up like a rush-hour traffic-jam in the heart of Manhattan. Was he out of line to bring up their past? He had questions that deserved answers. If nothing else, he'd gain closure.

Seeing a piece of gray driftwood floating in the surf, Tradd walked closer, snatching it from the water and pitching it farther into the ocean.

Mary watched from across the beanery as Sunlyn swept the floor with vigor. Shaking her head, Mary crossed the café, placing her hand on the broom and causing Sunlyn to stop.

"What has gotten into you?"

"What?" Sunlyn barked.

"Let go of the broom before you snap it in half. I've never seen you sweep the floor like that."

Calm flowed over Sunlyn as she relinquished the broom. "I'm sorry. I didn't mean to bite your head off."

"No worries. What's gotten you so upset?"

"No one." She shook her head. "Nothing."

Mary pursed her lips while leaning the broom against the counter. "Let's try this again. Who is under your skin?"

"Tradd Morrison," Sunlyn blurted before she could stop herself.

Mary palmed her forehead. "Of course!"

"Wait. Why would you say that?"

"I mean, it's obvious he's the one that has you so unnerved."

"Yeah, right. That'll be the day Tradd Morrison has that effect over me." Sunlyn walked behind the counter and poured herself a cup of coffee. "Tradd Morrison, ha!"

Mary strolled behind the counter and poured herself a cup of coffee too. "Listen, I didn't just roll in with the tide this morning. Every time you two run into each other this is your reaction. What gives? Dish."

Mary studied Sunlyn's expression. She and Sunlyn had been friends for 15 years. Mary knew her like a book. And occasionally over the years, she heard Tradd's name come up in conversation. Whenever it did, Sunlyn would act weird.

Mary and Sunlyn had met at the Beach Bum Beanery years ago, when Mary and her husband Ryan had moved to Sunset Beach. Ryan had accepted a position as manager of the Sandpiper Country Club in Calabash. Mary began looking for a part-time job. Even though at the time Sunlyn didn't know it, her uncle was ill, and the extra help came in handy. Hiring Mary also enabled Sunlyn to spend more time with her uncle before his passing.

Mary sipped her coffee while sizing-up Sunlyn. Her friend had an air of nervousness, fidgeting with the case of baked goods, switching their trays on the display shelves as if it made a world of difference.

Sunlyn met Mary's eyes. Mary raised her eyebrows expectantly.

Sunlyn groaned and rolled her eyes.

"Look. We, meaning Tradd and I, go back a long time. First, we were friends, then we dated, and then . . ."

"Then what?"

"Well, he made a zillion plans for us and our future, and I . . . well . . . I had a change of heart."

Mary gave her friend a quizzical look. "Change of heart about what?"

"Him. School. The restaurant. You name it." Sunlyn straightened from the display case and shrugged.

"What happened?"

"I stayed here, and he went away to school. In Canada."

"Oh."

"It's complicated," Sunlyn squeaked.

Mary tried sounding positive. "It doesn't have to be, does it? I mean, Tradd's back now—"

"—Yeah, to clean out his mother's house, then back to the Big Apple. But the complicated thing is that I ghosted him when he left for Canada."

Mary shook her head. "You *what* him?" she asked, voice hitched.

"I ghosted Tradd. Ignored all of his texts and phone calls."

"Why?"

"Like I said, it's complicated."

"Then uncomplicate it," Mary said brusquely. Reaching under the counter for her purse, Mary slung it over her shoulder. "My shift is over, unless you need me to stay longer?"

"No, you head home," Sunlyn said with a wave of her hand, dismissing her friend.

TEN

The following morning, as Sunlyn fidgeted with the beanery receipts from the day before, she looked up as the door to her shop opened and Tradd Morrison walked in. Letting her eyes linger for a few seconds longer than she should have, Sunlyn glanced away when she realized he'd noticed her looking.

He hadn't changed much in twenty years. Same brown, curly hair and dark, almost black, eyes. His cheeks were a little fuller than before, but the same undeniable cute and perfectly round dimples remained as she remembered. Sunlyn used to love staring into his eyes and getting lost in those dimples when he smiled or laughed.

"I have an idea," Tradd spoke, cutting into her musings.

"What's that?"

"I boxed up the things in my mother's kitchen and got to thinking, why not let you come over and go through her baking pans and things."

Sunlyn shrugged. "I don't know. . ."

"I'm not keeping them. I planned on donating them somewhere, but if you could use them for the coffee shop . . . well . . . why not?"

He did have a point. Thinking, Sunlyn tapped a pen off her chin. Some of her muffin and cake pans had seen better days. What would it hurt?

"I suppose I could take a look at them, if, you're sure."

"Absolutely."

"I'm the only one at the beanery today, so I could stop by after I close."

Suddenly two dimples emerged on his cheeks, and Tradd chuckled.

"What's funny?"

"You," Tradd said. He wet his finger with his tongue and then rubbed that finger on her chin. "Next time, make sure the tip of your pen is retracted." He reached, taking the pen from her hand, and pushed the button to close it.

"Oh." Sunlyn's cheeks warmed with the embarrassment or was it from the feel of his thumb brushing against her? "Thank you." Either way, it didn't matter.

"Great. It's a date."

"It's not a date," Sunlyn protested. "It's just a business transaction."

"A business transaction," Tradd said with distaste.

Sunlyn nodded. "Yes. A business transaction." Her arms folded in front of her.

Tradd's brows knitted together. "You can call it whatever you want, but it's a date." He turned and strode across the shop. Opening the door, he turned, looking back at her. "Make sure you're hungry. I'll whip something together for dinner."

Before she could protest, Sunlyn watched Tradd walk through the door, closing it behind him, leaving no room to object to the dinner.

Sunlyn took a deep breath as she locked the beanery for the night. Was she making a mistake about seeing Tradd? The summer's humidity still hung in the air early into the evening hours. No breezes today. After being cooped up in the shop all day, Sunlyn decided to walk to Tradd's house.

Arriving at Tradd's a few minutes later, Sunlyn glanced toward Sunset Inn. Andrea was leaving for the day. They smiled and waved. Sunlyn chuckled again about how she and Tradd had first met, climbed the steps, and knocked on his door.

Tradd answered right away with a wide grin.

"Come in," he said, stepping aside.

Sunlyn stepped inside the kitchen she was all too familiar with. She and Tradd had spent many hours creating new recipes to try. Stopping near the kitchen island, stacked with boxes, her mind drifted back.

They had declared their intentions to be a famous chef and pastry chef in this kitchen. Sunlyn wanted her own bakery, with a line out the door and around the corner.

Tradd had suggested a restaurant instead. And wanted a pinky promise to go with the idea.

Sunlyn had thrown flour in his face instead. They were only 16. How could she have promised any such thing to him?

She'd gotten a face full of breadcrumbs for her trouble.

Tradd touched her arm now, and she jerked as if his fingers were hot.

"Are you alright?" Tradd asked.

Sunlyn blinked a few times to bring her thoughts back to the present. "Sorry. Just fine."

"Where were you? You seemed like a million miles away."

"I was remembering the time we threw flour and breadcrumbs at each other—"

"—I remember that."

"And your mom couldn't even pretend to be mad. She was the greatest. She always believed in you."

Tradd cleared his throat. "As mothers go, she was pretty awesome."

The sound of food sizzling in the skillet captured their attention while the smell of garlic and shrimp teased their senses.

"I'd better tend to dinner. All the boxes with her kitchen stuff are stacked over there." He pointed to a stack lined up against the wall. "Look through them and take whatever you want."

Sunlyn smiled. "Thanks, but I walked here. Can I set aside whatever I want and grab them another day?"

"You've got it. I'm making shrimp scampi. I thought it would be nice to eat outside on the deck as the sun sets."

"That sounds lovely."

After finishing dinner, Tradd took their plates back inside and returned with two glasses of red wine. "How about an after-dinner drink?"

As she reached to take the glass, Sunlyn's fingers brushed against Tradd's. Shivers traveled up her arm. Why? After twenty years and living several states away, Tradd shouldn't still be able to cause that type of reaction within.

"I've forgotten how much I enjoy watching the sun set over the saltmarsh." Tradd sat next to Sunlyn. "Just look at those pinks, oranges, and yellows. It's absolutely perfect the way they fade into blue and then disappear."

Sunlyn took a sip of her wine. "Are they that different from New York?"

"Not different. Running my restaurant doesn't give me much time to enjoy the sunsets. Or the sunrises, for that matter."

"That's too bad . . ." Sunlyn let her voice trail off, listening to the rapid series of chickenlike clucks coming from the marsh, followed by what sounded like laughter. "Tell me . . . what bird is making that sound?"

Tradd closed his eyes, listening for a few seconds. "Purple gallinules." He sheepishly smiled, eyeing Sunlyn.

Sunlyn glanced over at him. "That's amazing how you can do that."

Those dimples!

Was it her imagination, or was it warmer outside now than it was earlier? Perhaps it was the wine making her temperature rise. Perhaps. She knew better, though. Sunlyn knew all too well that it was Tradd's dimples.

Raising her glass, Sunlyn sipped her wine, trying to find her comfort zone again. "I'm definitely spoiled living on Sunset Beach."

A serious look washed across Tradd's face. "You've never lived anywhere else? Always here?"

"Uh-huh." Her voice was low.

She knew where this conversation was heading. And that was a road she wasn't sure she wanted to visit again. At least not tonight. Eventually. One day. Maybe. She could feel his eyes on her, waiting for more of an answer.

"How long have you been in New York?" Would the diversion tactic work?

He shrugged. "I opened The Gathering Place 10 years ago."

"Wait. What?" Sunlyn downed the last of her wine. Was it for courage? How could he? "You stuck with the name?" Sunlyn rubbed the back of her neck as the heat settled, and it wasn't from the humidity.

How was she supposed to react to that? Was she supposed to react? She was the one who had stayed behind. Plans changed. People changed. But the name of the restaurant that you were supposed to own and manage together . . . didn't change.

"I . . . um . . . well . . . yes." Tradd stumbled over his words.

Sunlyn stood. "It's getting late," she stammered abruptly as her hand rubbed her forehead.

"I'll walk you home."

"I don't need an escort, but thank you."

"I don't mind."

"This isn't New York. I'll be fine."

"I insist. I wouldn't feel right knowing you were walking by yourself in the dark."

Sunlyn stared at Tradd. Sure, he felt bad about her walking home but not about naming his restaurant the same as *their* restaurant. Wasn't there some kind of code about that sort of thing? What was wrong with her? Why was she even upset?

She sighed. "Well, since you insist."

The two of them walked in silence, guided by the moon. As they approached her beach house the sounds of the tumbling surf filled the air.

Sunlyn turned toward Tradd. "Well, here we are. Thank you for walking me home."

"You are welcome."

Sunlyn's eyes glazed over Tradd. He looked as if he was going to say something. He didn't. Instead, his knuckles caressed her cheek. Sunlyn froze, knowing what was coming next. Tradd leaned in, and his lips brushed over hers.

The kiss was soft at first, almost undetectable by Sunlyn, then intensified as if their kissing was an everyday occurrence. Needing something to steady herself, Sunlyn let her hands come to rest on Tradd's arms as she kissed him back.

Becoming lost in his kiss, Sunlyn felt her nerves becoming jangled instead of enjoying the moment.

She pushed off his arms and took a few steps backward.

"I . . ." Sunlyn whispered, her fingers landing on her lips. "I can't do this," she blurted. Turning, she rushed up the steps and into her house.

ELEVEN

Mary eyed Sunlyn rushing into the Beach Bum Beanery the following morning with an armful of containers. Drying her hands on her apron, Mary grabbed a couple of the containers from Sunlyn's arms as they teetered, threatening to fall to the floor.

"What's going on with you?" Mary asked, setting the containers on top of the display case.

"What do you mean?"

"I mean, did you look in the mirror this morning? I think you forgot to brush your hair."

Sunlyn shook her head. "No, I didn't. I was up all-night baking."

"You're kidding." Mary peered closer and pointed toward Sunlyn's eyes. "That explains the dark circles. Come." Mary latched on to her boss' arm and guided Sunlyn toward a table in the corner. "Sit. I'll pour the coffee."

"What? No. Who has time to sit? I have things to do."

"Coffee first, before you fall over."

Sunlyn sat down with a large sigh.

Mary was back at the table in a minute, with two mugs of coffee. "I thought you were taking the morning off since you were here all day yesterday. What happened?"

"Nothing. I couldn't sleep. So, I decided to experiment. I made dark-chocolate-espresso muffins, more peanut butter cups, and several different flavors of scones."

"Impressive. Espresso muffins, huh?" Mary's eyebrows shot upward.

"They're for the customers," Sunlyn said, pointing at her friend.

Mary stuck her hands up in the air. "Okay, okay." Picking up her mug, she glanced over the rim at Sunlyn while taking a sip. "I don't think I've ever seen you like this—"

"—Like what?"

"Disheveled."

"It's nothing, really. I mean, it was only one kiss." Sunlyn took a long sip of the coffee. "It didn't mean anything."

"He kissed you!" Mary practically yelled. "Wait. You are talking about Tradd, right?"

Sunlyn's lips pursed. "Of course I'm talking about Tradd. Who else?"

"I'm sorry, but this involves chocolate. Chocolate-espresso-brownies, to be exact. I'll be right back." Mary shot up, rushed behind the counter, and snatched two muffins from the container. Sitting back at the table, she placed them on napkins and slid one in the direction of Sunlyn. "Start talking."

"Hey, these are for the customers!"

"Are you kidding me? You must have 50 of these. I don't think the beanery will miss two."

"Fine." Sunlyn rolled her eyes while taking a bite of the muffin. "Tradd stopped by the shop yesterday, wanting to know if I wanted his mother's baking pans and such—"

"—And," Mary interrupted.

Rolling her eyes, Sunlyn jutted her chin at Mary. "As I was saying, after I closed up shop, I went over to Tradd's place—"

"—And," Mary said, leaning in closer.

Sunlyn took another sip of her coffee before continuing. "Well, to make a long story short . . . Tradd made dinner, we talked, and he walked me home."

"And!"

"I swear, Mary, you're more excited about him kissing me than I was."

"You weren't excited?"

"I'd say surprised."

"Then, what happened?"

"I kind of kissed him back." Sunlyn slouched down in her chair. "What was I thinking?"

"That maybe you enjoyed him kissing you, so you kissed him back." Mary's brows raised in question.

Both of Sunlyn's palms covered her face. "That's the problem," she muttered behind her palms, then lowered them, crossing her arms over her chest. "He lives in New York, and I live here."

"So?"

"So, why even start something? As soon as he clears out his mother's house, he's on the first plane out of here." Sunlyn straightened, running her fingers through her hair. "And." She pointed at her friend. "He named his restaurant the name of *our* restaurant." Sunlyn pushed up from her chair, grabbing her coffee mug. "Seriously, who does that?"

"Um. Well . . ." Mary winced.

"What?" Sunlyn drained the last of her coffee and sat down again.

"You ghosted him. What was he supposed to do, give up on his dream just because you did?"

Sunlyn's mouth gaped. "But—"

Mary's eyes narrowed.

"I—"

Mary laced her fingers together on top of the table. "Are you finished?"

Sunlyn shrugged.

"You need to talk to Tradd. Let him know what you're feeling."

"I . . . can't," Sunlyn replied.

Mary took a sip of her coffee. "Why not?"

"Because, don't you get it? I feel guilty about ghosting him, and now he's back and thinks he can just pick up where we left off."

"Can't you?"

"I don't even know what that is."

Mary stood, collecting the mugs and muffin wrappers from the table. "Then, don't you think it's time to find out?"

Around noon Tradd took a break from packing the house, grabbed a cold bottle of beer from the refrigerator, and sat on the back deck. Sitting, he pulled his phone from his shirt pocket and called Mitch.

"Boss, what's up?"

"As long as things are running smoothly, I think I'll stay a little longer."

"Oh. Sure. Things are good here. How's it going at Sunset Beach?"

"It was only one kiss," Tradd said without thinking.

"Who's talking about kissing?" Mitch asked.

"Wait. Why did you say kissing?"

"Hey, Tradd, I didn't say anything about kissing. You did."

"I did?" Tradd's hand raked through his hair. *Focus man.* "I guess I did."

"Who's the lucky lady?"

"No one. Sunlyn."

"*Thee* Sunlyn?" Mitch asked.

"Okay. Okay. No need for theatrics. It was just one kiss after I walked her home."

"You walked her home?"

"Yes, after we had dinner together."

"You had dinner together?"

"What is this? You sound like a parrot."

Mitch roared with laughter. "Just surprised. I thought you were just packing up your mom's stuff, and now you're dating your old flame."

Tradd took a swig of beer. "Slow it down. I'm not seeing Sunlyn. It was just dinner and a walk."

"And a kiss," Mitch added.

"And a kiss," Tradd confirmed. "Besides, it's not going anywhere. I live there, and she lives here."

"Uh-huh."

"Is that all you have to say?"

"No."

"What, then?"

"You can do better than using where you live as an excuse. Because in today's world, the distance between here and there, is under two hours by plane."

Tradd grumbled, knowing Mitch was right. Just then he heard a loud crash and shattering glass. "What was that?" Tradd asked, eager to change the subject.

Mitch sucked in his breath. "That, I'm guessing, would be the new waitress. I have her stacking the water goblets. She's a bit of a klutz at times."

"From the sound of it, we have a lot fewer glasses than we did a few minutes ago."

"Yeah, I'd better lend a hand."

"Good idea. I'll call you in a few days." Tradd swiped the end icon on his phone.

Two wood storks caught his eye, flying from the saltmarsh. They flew in sync, swooping and swaying gracefully above the marsh until they were out of sight.

If things were only as simple as a short plane ride away. Tradd brought the beer to his lips, taking a long gulp. Remembering Sunlyn's words from the evening before, he shook his head.

Why couldn't she do this? What even was it that she couldn't do?

Kiss him? Because if that was the case, she'd done it, and it was just as he remembered, soft and sweet. No. Wait. Her kisses were better than that. Familiar and welcoming.

Weren't they connected at the hip, everyone said?

Of course, that was a long time ago. Too many years had elapsed for that to still be a thing. Could things be that simple as to reconnect and pick up where they had left off twenty years ago?

Tradd guessed it could. If that's what they both wanted.

He did.

Did Sunlyn?

TWELVE

Sunlyn sat with her legs splayed onto the hard-packed sand, letting the rolling tide wash over them. She smiled as a trio of sandpipers ran back and forth with the tide.

"Good morning, Larry, Moe, Curly." Reaching, she grabbed a handful of sand, letting it sift through her fingers like the sands in an hourglass. "You little guys don't know how good you have it. I mean, look at you. You just run around on the beach all day. The only care in the world is finding a treat in the sand." Sunlyn sighed, closing her eyes, and tilted her head upward to let the afternoon sun warm her face.

Just as her shoulders relaxed, a cool shadow blocked the sun. She opened her eyes and squinted. Tradd loomed above her, both hands shoved into his pockets.

Her heart dropped into her stomach.

He sat beside her and cracked a smile. "From where I'm sitting, you don't have it too bad either," he said, bringing his knees up to his chest and resting his arms on them.

"I didn't know anyone was behind me." Sunlyn's face tinted to a light shade of pink.

"I don't think that would have stopped you. For as long as I can remember you talked to the sandpipers."

Sunlyn stared into his dark eyes, missing him. Although, she would never admit that. His life was in New York. "Probably not. Sandpipers are my beady-eyed therapists."

"I just dropped off your box of baking supplies at the beanery. Mary said I'd probably find you here."

"My favorite place." Sunlyn forced her gaze to pivot from Tradd's eyes to the sandpipers.

"I'm staying a little longer."

"You are?" He had her attention now. "For how long?"

"At least another week, maybe two. I want to paint the inside of the beach house—"

"—Oh."

"Look, I'm sorry that I made things weird by kissing you last night. It's just—with the moon glimmering in your hair—"

"—The kiss was totally unexpected. But that's not what made things weird." An ocean breeze kicked up, blowing Sunlyn's hair onto her face. Before she knew what was happening, Tradd reached over and brushed it from her cheeks, tucking a wisp behind her ear. Swallowing hard, she forced her eyes to meet Tradd's.

"What, then?" he asked.

"It's not just one thing. I mean," Sunlyn stared into the ocean.

"I can't fix it if you don't tell me," Tradd coaxed.

"Why did you name your restaurant the name of our restaurant?" Sunlyn's eyes returned to his face, studying it like a map. Looking for lines or creases of admission.

Tradd jumped to his feet and extended his hands toward Sunlyn. "I feel like walking."

Accepting his hands, Sunlyn walked with him. "It's a fair-enough question," she said.

"Why do you care?" he asked pointedly.

"Excuse me?"

"Why do you care? You canceled our plans last minute, no heads up."

"I told you I needed to stay and help my uncle."

"You never answered my calls or texts. Why?"

"I . . ." How was she supposed to answer that? Perhaps it was time. She could finally let go of the guilt. Finally get the answers she needed, as well.

Sunlyn stopped, grabbing Tradd's hand. He stopped too, and she guided his face to meet hers. "You planned everything for us. By yourself."

Tradd's Adam's apple bobbed in his throat, and he blinked at her words.

"I didn't have a say in anything."

"But—"

Sunlyn held up her index finger, signaling for him to stop. "—What was I supposed to do? Tell me. That night, on the beach, after I told you, we walked to the Kindred Spirit, to write in the journal—" Her hand came to rest at her side.

"—I remember."

"I spilled my heart about our future together. Do you remember what you wrote?"

"Come on, Sunlyn, do you really expect me to remember that?"

"Yes, I do. After you walked me home, I went back. I had to know—"

"—Know what?"

"I had to know what you wrote." Sunlyn balled her fists at her sides. "You wrote about how excited you were about school in Canada and your plans."

"So, what's wrong with that?"

"It was supposed to be about us, Tradd. Our plans. Not your plans. You never included me in what you wrote."

Flinging his arms from his side, Tradd stepped back with frustration. "You're kidding, right? You didn't go with me to Canada because of my word choices?"

"We were planning our lives together. So, yes, partly that. And partly from what you didn't say."

Tradd scrubbed his chin. "What didn't I say?"

A rumble sounded in the sky above them, and she noticed the dark clouds for the first time.

"You expected me to just leave my life here on the island, and you couldn't even say . . ."

"—Say what?"

The wind picked up, blowing Sunlyn's hair in every direction. Reaching, she peeled the strands from her face. "You never once said that you loved me. Yet, I was supposed to follow you to another country?"

"I didn't need to say it. We were best friends from the moment we crashed our bikes."

A loud crack of thunder startled Sunlyn as the waves rushed ashore with vengeance, causing them to step farther back into the looser sand.

"We weren't just best friends," Sunlyn answered.

"I know."

Sunlyn's eyes narrowed. "Look, I was wrong to not take your calls. I needed to find out if you loved me."

"I did."

"I waited. I listened to your messages, thinking that maybe, just maybe, you would at least tell me over the phone. You never did."

A flash of lightning tore through the sky.

"Then your calls stopped." Sunlyn shrugged. "I had my answer."

"No. You're wrong."

"We need to go. It's not safe on the beach during a storm," Sunlyn yelled above the howling wind. "Do what you have to do at your mom's house." Her brows knitted together with sadness. "New York is waiting."

In the next beat, Sunlyn turned on her heels, rushing from the beach and willing herself not to look back at Tradd.

THIRTEEN

The following morning Mary arrived at the Beach Bum Beanery to find Sunlyn already sweeping debris from the parking lot.

"That storm wreaked havoc, didn't it?"

Sunlyn looked at Mary. "Sure did. At least it wasn't a hurricane."

"True that," Mary mumbled. "How's your house?"

"Pretty good. A few pieces of siding blew off, but that's about it. What about your place?"

"Came through unscathed. I can't say the same for the Sandpiper Country Club. And it's on the mainland! There are tree branches and leaves littered across the golf course. Ryan left early to start the clean-up process."

The two of them walked inside the shop.

Mary turned on the lights. "Ryan said he'd help fix any damage to the coffee shop and your house."

"That would be great. Storms sure can be strange, can't they?" Sunlyn asked, slipping her apron over her head and tying it behind her back.

"That's a fact," Mary agreed.

"I imagine we'll be busy this morning after the storm last night. People will probably skip making breakfast at home and just grab something here, before jumping right into cleaning," Sunlyn said, while brewing the coffee.

Mary nodded and started filling the napkin dispensers that sat on the tables.

Sunlyn didn't know where she'd be without her friendship with Mary and Ryan. They'd been there for her from day one, 15 years ago. Sunlyn smiled, thinking back to the day she'd met Mary.

Mary had cut a strange picture when she bounced into the coffee shop that day—black hair cut in pixie style, and with the ends dyed in pink. It had been a cheerful sight, especially since Sunlyn had been up all night worrying about what results the doctors would announce from the battery of tests they'd put her uncle through. Uncle Tom couldn't work, and Sunlyn had just braved the morning coffee rush by herself.

Mary had stood on the other side of the counter, extended her hand, and asked if Sunlyn might be hiring. Just part-time.

Sunlyn couldn't pass up that opportunity. Especially once she'd received the bad news from Tom Bean's doctor. Mary's working had enabled Sunlyn to spend more time with Tom before he passed.

"Sunlyn, did you hear me?" Mary asked, walking toward her.

"I'm sorry, I was just thinking."

"I take it Tradd found you yesterday." Mary pointed to the box of baking pans on the floor near the back door.

Sunlyn smirked. "Yep."

"And . . ."

"You could say we talked."

"Did you guys clear the air? I like him. I think he's good for you."

"How can you say that? You don't even know him." Sunlyn's tone was dry, but her heart fluttered.

"That's why." Mary slipped on her apron.

"What?"

"I say that because of your reaction. Every time you talk with him, or I mention his name, you get flustered."

"I do not!"

"Point in case," Mary said.

The door opened, and Tradd Morrison strolled in. "I need coffee and lots of it," he said, without smiling.

Sunlyn looked at him. Dark circles under his eyes, hair disheveled. And no dimples. "What's going on? You look terrible."

"Gee, thanks. Nice to see you too," he muttered.

"Just saying." Sunlyn held up a to-go cup in one hand and a thermos in her other. "What'll it be?"

"Thermos. That storm was nasty, wasn't it?"

"Just be glad it wasn't a hurricane. It's the season for them."

Tradd grunted. "Might as well have been."

Sunlyn cocked her head. "What do you mean?"

"I now have four holes in my roof."

Sunlyn gasped. "Oh no!"

"Yep. I spent the night emptying buckets. I don't suppose you could recommend a roof guy?"

Sunlyn thought for a minute while tucking a strand of hair behind her ear. "Try Calabash Contracting. They put the roof on this place a few years back."

"I'll look into them." Tradd paid for his thermos of coffee and strode out.

Mary's phone rang in her pocket, then just as it started ringing, it stopped. Mary pulled it out of her pocket. "That's weird."

"What is?" Sunlyn asked while making another pot of coffee.

"Ryan just called. He usually never calls me while he's working."

"You'd better call him back."

"I think you're right." Mary hit the call icon next to his name and stepped outside.

A group of six men walked in and sat at two tables. Sunlyn strolled over to their tables and smiled. "What can I get you?"

"We're all together," the man said, motioning to both tables. "I get the check. Lots of coffee. Black. And how about an assortment of breakfast muffins, or whatever you have."

"Coming right up. Do you guys have damage from the storm?"

"How'd you know? We all live on the same block and decided to tackle one house at a time. Maybe we'll get it done faster if we work together."

Sunlyn smiled. "Good idea. I'll be right back with your order. I just brewed a fresh pot of coffee." Sunlyn walked behind the counter and started filling mugs with coffee as Mary came back inside. Her face looked ashen.

"Everything okay?" Sunlyn inquired.

Mary shook her head. "I'm not sure. Let's tend to the customers. Then we'll talk."

Thirty minutes later, Sunlyn and Mary sat at one of the tables near the front window, each with a mug of coffee.

Sunlyn spoke first. "What did Ryan want?"

Mary took a long sip of coffee before answering. "He told me the owners of the country club scheduled a meeting with him this evening," she said, taking a deep breath. "It turns out, they're impressed with his management skills and want to speak with him about managing their new country club."

"That's wonderful," Sunlyn chimed, then noticed the worried look appearing across Mary's face. "Isn't it?"

"It depends on how you look at it."

"Why? Where's the new club going to be?"

"Seattle," Mary mumbled.

"Wait a minute." Sunlyn shook her head. "I must have heard you wrong. Where?"

Mary's hands steepled over her nose and mouth. "Seattle," she muffled.

Sunlyn set her mug on the table with a loud thud, causing coffee to slosh over the rim. "Seattle, Washington?" She leaned back in her chair, with the wind knocked out of her.

"The one and only."

Sunlyn's ears began ringing, and she sucked in a breath. This wasn't happening. Was it?

Sunlyn couldn't bear to lose another person in her life. First her parents, then Tradd, and then her uncle. She'd never had a friend for as long as she'd known Mary. When would it stop?

An uncomfortable, unsafe feeling started balling in the bottom of her stomach. She hadn't felt it for so long. *Not again.*

Mary's hand stretched across the table, landing on Sunlyn's, gently squeezing. "I'm meeting Ryan for a quick dinner before his meeting later. I'll know more then."

Sunlyn squeezed Mary's hand back. "Let's meet at the Milk and Honey afterward. You can fill me in."

Mary stood. "Sounds like a plan."

FOURTEEN

Sunlyn hadn't expected the Milk and Honey Restaurant and Bar to be so busy on a weeknight. Her eyes searched through the crowd for Mary. Her friend sat at a small table across the restaurant.

Waving hello, Sunlyn crossed the room. Her steps felt heavy, almost as if she was trying to walk in quicksand. Her stomach protested too, swirling in circles, like the kind she'd get after riding the Tilt-A-Whirl ride at the county fair.

Slumping into the chair across from Mary, Sunlyn took one look at Mary's crestfallen face and knew the answer.

"That bad, huh?" Sunlyn asked.

Mary nodded.

"When?"

"We leave at the end of next month." The waiter appeared with a variety basket of fried food: mushrooms, mozzarella sticks, pickle slices, and French fries. The waiter also set two raspberry mimosas on the table.

Sunlyn's eyes grew wide.

Mary shrugged. "I stressed ordered for us."

Sunlyn didn't want to eat. But she took a long sip from her glass. "Is this for real? Maybe the position is temporary. You know, just to get the place up and running."

"I wish." Mary nibbled on a mushroom. "It's permanent."

"I can't believe it." Sunlyn's heart clenched. "What am I going to do without you?"

"I know." Mary grabbed a cheese stick. "It won't be the same, but at least we can video chat."

The waiter reappeared with two additional mimosas.

"Wait." Mary stopped him. "We didn't order these."

"I know." Pointing toward the man at the far end of the bar, the waiter spoke. "He did," he said, then moved to another table.

Sunlyn's head turned in the direction the waiter had pointed.

"Tradd Morrison!" Mary whispered.

"Unbelievable," Sunlyn mumbled under her breath. "He's like a bad penny."

"Why don't you go talk to him?"

"No way. I'm here with you," Sunlyn barked.

"I'm not much company. Go ahead." Mary stood. "I'll see you at the beanery tomorrow."

"Are you sure?"

Mary nodded. Laying enough money on the table to cover the bill, she left.

"This is just great," Sunlyn sputtered. This was not the way she'd hoped the evening would end. At this moment, the last person she wanted to run into was Tradd. Was he following her? How could they both end up at the same place, especially with him not knowing the local places?

Taking Mary's advice, Sunlyn stood, all the while aware of Tradd's eyes watching her every move. Toying with the idea of making a quick dash for the door, she instead heaved a big sigh and squared her shoulders. Why put off the inevitable? Mary would want the details the next day at work. There was no getting out of it. Sunlyn headed toward Tradd and sat on the empty barstool next to him.

Taking a sip of her drink, Sunlyn spoke. "What are you doing here?"

"Enjoying my evening." Tradd's eyes narrowed. "I could ask the same of you."

"Touché." The hum of chatter filled the establishment encircling them. "Thanks for the drink."

"You're welcome." Tradd took a sip of his beer while drumming his fingers off the top of the bar's counter. He turned in his seat, looking at Sunlyn. "Look, we're not kids any more. Can we call a truce?"

Sunlyn smiled slightly, unsure.

"For old-time's sake?" Tradd asked again.

She blew out a puff of hot air. "Fine." She was sure they could get along for however long he was on the island. After all, it was temporary and then they'd both go back to their corners of the world and life would go on as normal.

Tradd grabbed a handful of peanuts from the basket sitting on the bar.

"Did you call Calabash Contracting?"

"Yep." He hurriedly finished chewing. "They're stopping by tomorrow to assess the damage."

"Good." Sunlyn reached up, rubbing her neck, the conversation awkward. Would this ever get easier?

"Would you like to dance?" Tradd asked.

"But . . . but . . . there's no music."

"There's a juke box over there." He pointed toward it. "What do you say?"

"Honestly, I can't remember the last time I danced."

"I'll take it." Tradd jumped from his stool, pulling a handful of coins from his pocket. Taking a few minutes to preview the playlist, he found the perfect song. Their song. He deposited a few coins in and pressed S8 for the song.

A few minutes later Sunlyn almost choked on her drink. *Their* song. He'd picked it. Blood pounded in her ears as Tradd turned from the jukebox, fixed his eyes on hers, and held out his hand to her.

She stepped away from the bar and took his hand. Her breath caught in her throat.

Why did he have to pick this song?

Closing her eyes, Sunlyn tried blocking out the song and the memories it evoked.

"Do you remember?" Tradd asked.

Sunlyn nodded, not trusting herself to speak. Too many memories bubbled, threatening to overflow.

Tradd pulled her closer, and her throat constricted. Her breathing felt labored. Her eyes flew open as she stepped from Tradd's arms.

"I can't breathe," Sunlyn whispered, her hand coming to her chest. Her heart rate felt ragged. "I . . . can't. I'm sorry." Her ears began ringing.

Panic settled in, flowing through her veins. It was too late to stop it. Sunlyn's eyes swept through the crowd of people enjoying themselves. Everyone except her. Even Tradd was enjoying their time together.

Catching a glimpse of the exit sign hanging above the door, Sunlyn made her escape.

Tradd stood rigid, stunned at Sunlyn's reaction. What had just happened? His feet remained glued to the wooden floor. Willing them to move, he chased after Sunlyn.

His heart stopped as he found Sunlyn outside, palms resting on her knees, gasping for air. Reaching her, Tradd grabbed her shoulders and spun her around to face him. Tears stained her cheeks.

"Sunlyn, talk to me. What's wrong?"

"The song . . ."

"What about it? It never made you cry before." His hands cupped her face, his thumbs brushing her tears. "You're scaring me." His arms slid around Sunlyn, holding her tight. "Sunlyn," he tenderly said her name.

"It's wrong . . . the—" she sobbed between words— "song . . ."

Tradd stroked her hair, more confused than ever. "How?"

She sniffled, her breathing calmed. Her eyes peered deeply into Tradd's. He saw her swallow hard.

"Don't you get it?" she asked. "We don't have all the time in the world. We're not 18 anymore. We're 38. The world continues to spin forward, taking us with it." Sunlyn swiped at a lone tear and turned away from him. "Mary's leaving me. Just like everyone else. I feel like my heart is shrinking from losing so many people, and soon there won't be anything left—"

"—Mary's leaving? Why?"

"Her husband's job transferred him to the West Coast."

"I'm sorry, Sunlyn." He wished he could erase her pain. He couldn't. "I'm here."

"Are you really?"

"Of course, I am."

"But you're not. Not really. I mean, sure, for the time being, but soon you'll be leaving. Your life is in New York."

"Come with me, then."

She stiffened, then turned to look at him. "What?" Her face looked incredulous. Was he really asking that much? Her life was on Sunset Beach.

He plunged ahead. "Come with me. We can work together at The Gathering Place. Side by side. Just like we'd planned."

Tradd watched as Sunlyn's face cork-screwed. She closed her eyes and then schooled her face. All the signs of her deep thought process. What was going on in that complex mind of hers? His hand reached down catching hers.

"What do you think?" he asked, caressing her hand. "Let me show you New York."

"I—" her mouth opened, then closed.

"You're going to love it. New York is nothing like Sunset Beach. It's bustling with people everywhere you turn, not to mention the theater district—"

"—But my home is on Sunset Beach. I just can't pick up and leave. What about my shop?"

Tradd twisted his face as he shrugged. "Sell it."

"'Sell it?'"

"You'll be working with me. You won't need it."

"I can't sell my uncle's place." Sunlyn's voice hitched.

"Why not? He's been gone a long time. Why are you still letting him run your life? Hasn't your prison sentence been long enough?"

As soon as Tradd spoke those words, he wished he could take them back. The glimmer of light faded in her eyes. She wouldn't leave. Their time had passed. There was no recapturing the past and picking up where they'd left things.

An expression he had never seen before washed over Sunlyn's face. Without saying a word, she turned, unlocked her car door, climbed in, and drove away.

Tradd stood in the parking lot, watching, until he could no longer see the lights of her car. He watched those sunset promises they had made to one another twenty years ago fade with her.

FIFTEEN

Still standing in the parking lot, Tradd scrubbed his face quietly, hoping Sunlyn would change her mind, turn her car around, and drive back to him.

She didn't.

Now what was he supposed to do? There'd be no sleeping tonight.

His comment about "'prison'" was out of line. Who was he to judge why she'd stayed in Sunset Beach all these years? Though, living a life for someone else was no way to live. Tradd strode back into the bar. Reclaiming his seat, he noticed their drinks were still there.

He motioned for the bartender and ordered a beer.

"Will your date be joining you again?" the bartender asked.

"Afraid not," Tradd replied, keeping his eyes on the counter.

"Wanna talk about it?"

"Not much to say." Tradd picked up his beer, taking a long swig. "We dated once—a lifetime ago. I was hoping we could pick up where we left off." Tradd reached toward the basket of peanuts, grabbing a handful. "She's not thrilled about that idea."

The bartender slapped his hand off the top of the bar counter. "I've heard it all, working here. Can I give you a piece of advice?"

"Sure." Tradd dropped the handful of peanuts into his mouth.

"Stop trying to pick up where you left off. Twenty years is a long time. You're older now. People change." He leaned in. "Swoon her, and start again."

"Huh? Swoon her?" Tradd's lip quirked.

"Yes. As if you just met. Get to know her again. Date her."

Tradd's eyes lit up. Standing on the rungs of the bar stool, he reached across the bar, cupping the bartender's face. "That's a magnificent idea!" Tradd kissed both of the man's cheeks and then plopped back onto the barstool. "Why didn't I think of that?"

Grunting, the bartender wiped his cheeks with the towel that hung on his shoulder. "Because you're too close to the subject to see the obvious."

Tradd nodded, swallowing the last of his beer. "Looks like I have some work to do." Reaching into his pocket, he pulled out some money for a tip, tossing it on the counter. "I'll see you later."

Tradd had a new spring in his step leaving the Milk and Honey. Something as simple as swooning. What had he been doing? He knew. He'd had his head in the clouds, or, more appropriately, in the kitchen. His all-consuming dream.

Perhaps it was time for a change. Sure, he had his dream, but what else? He was alone, and what good was achieving his dreams if he had no one to share them with at the end of the day? Someone to love.

First things first, Tradd thought as he drove home. He owed Sunlyn an apology.

Sunlyn cringed as Tradd walked into her shop the next morning. Folding her arms, she shook her head.

"What are you doing here?" she asked, deadpanned.

Inwardly Tradd smiled. His dentist greeted him with more excitement than Sunlyn did. He'd expected this. And it was okay with him. Tradd wanted a front-row seat for the events that were about to unfold.

"Coffee. I came for a large coffee and a couple of muffins," he said.

Sunlyn waved her arm toward the tables. "Fine," she said, tapping her foot. "Sit anywhere."

"Don't mind if I do," he replied, smugly.

Sunlyn watched as Tradd strode across the small shop and sat near the front window. Pursing her lips, she went about preparing his order. What was he up to? Placing his items onto a tray, she crossed the room and set the tray on the table. "Do you want anything else?"

He looked at her and smiled. "Nope."

Sunlyn placed the receipt for his order onto the tray and went behind the counter. Where was Mary when she needed her?

Mary and Ryan were meeting with a realtor, wanting to place their beach house on the market as soon as possible. Sadness washed over Sunlyn, realizing that soon enough this shop without Mary would be the new normal. Sunlyn would be by herself. No one to cover for her so she could take off a morning or afternoon. No one to run interference when needed. She could hire someone else. But she didn't want to.

"Excuse me?" a voice asked.

Lost in her thoughts, Sunlyn hadn't seen the person approach the counter. Was she seeing things? Laughter bubbled inside her. The man standing on the other side of the counter had a handful of balloon strings.

"What in the world?"

"Are you Sunlyn Bean?"

"Um, yes . . ." Sunlyn answered, almost as if she was unsure herself. Her eyes darted from the colorful balloon strings to the balloons at the end of them. She counted three balloons, all in the shape of sandpipers.

"Then these are for you," the man said, relief washing across his face. "Do you know how difficult it is to load balloons like this into my car and then unload them and bring them inside?"

"Um, no . . ." she hesitantly answered.

"Well, trust me, you don't want to. Where do you want them?"

"I guess you can stash them in the corner." Sunlyn pointed opposite to where Tradd was sitting.

Rushing around the counter, she met the man in the corner. "These are beautiful. I love sandpipers. How about a coffee to go on the house?"

"Sure. The biggest size you offer, with cream and sugar. Please."

Sunlyn smiled. "Coming right up. By the way, isn't there a card or something? I mean, who sent these to me?"

The man shook his head. "Nope. The guy had a message, though. 'Larry, Mo, and Curly.'"

Sunlyn's head jerked in Tradd's direction.

Tradd smiled, raised his mug toward her, and took a sip.

Turning her attention back to the delivery man, Sunlyn went behind the counter to prepare his coffee, as promised, all the while wondering what she was going to say to Tradd Morrison. When she turned around to hand the man his to-go coffee, Sunlyn was taken aback to see that Tradd had left the beanery without saying one word to her.

The same scene played out during the next three mornings. Tradd would come into her coffee shop, order coffee and a pastry, watch as her surprise was delivered, then leave without so much as a peep. After the sandpiper balloons, Sunlyn received a basket filled with a bottle of wine and two wine glasses, followed by a cheese board with assorted cheeses, and finally a top-of-the-line espresso machine for the beanery.

The evening after receiving the espresso machine, Sunlyn and Mary were cleaning the beanery.

"What are you going to say to him?" Mary asked.

Stopping her sweeping, Sunlyn looked at Mary wiping off the tables. "You know, I've thought of a zillion things these last few days . . ."

"—But?" Mary interrupted.

"But now, I'm not so sure. It's weird. I know the gifts are from Tradd. I just can't figure out the reason behind them." Sunlyn shrugged.

"Are you going to keep them?"

A grin appeared on Sunlyn's face. "How could I not? They're all my favorite things."

"OMG!"

"What?" Sunlyn asked.

"You like him again, don't you?"

"That's absurd. I don't like him. I can't allow myself to like him again. Not after what he said to me the other night."

"What exactly did he say?"

Sunlyn shivered, remembering. She wanted to forget his words. They were hurtful. Heartless. "Basically, he said I was still letting my uncle run my life after all these years and that I was in a prison of sorts."

"I don't know how he could be so cruel," Mary chirped.

"I guess Mr. Manhattan . . . 'I own a restaurant' . . . thought he could bribe me with presents—"

"—Not quite. I was trying to apologize to you." A man's voice seeped through the locked screen door. "And I'd like to take you out."

Sunlyn and Mary jumped.

"Hmm . . . that's my cue to leave." Mary tossed the wet rag into the sink, grabbed her purse, and let herself out, while letting Tradd in at the same time.

Tradd crossed the room, stopping in front of Sunlyn. "I'm sorry, Sunlyn. I'd like to take you out for an evening."

"Tradd." Sunlyn's eyes met his. "I already told you—"

"—I don't want to pick up where we left off. I want to start right here, right now. We're both different people than we were twenty years ago."

Sunlyn's mouth fell open.

"What do you say? Second chance?"

SIXTEEN

Sunlyn released her hair from the barrel of the hot curling iron. After adding soft curls the whole way around her head, she threaded her fingers through her hair, fluffing it a bit. Reaching for the lonesome tube of lipstick she owned, yet barely wore, Sunlyn swiped the pink color across her lips.

"What am I doing?" she asked herself.

A knock sounded on her door. Taking a deep breath, she flipped off the bathroom light and went to answer the door.

She smiled at Tradd as she let him in, blowing out a quick breath of hot air, trying to calm her nerves. Tradd looked dashing in his trousers and button-down, turquoise-colored shirt; his curly hair was still wet from his shower. And the humidity this evening wouldn't help it to dry any time soon.

Nervous, she shifted her weight from one foot to the other as she watched Tradd's eyes roam over her light-gray sundress and sandals.

"You look beautiful, Sunlyn."

Feeling her cheeks warm, she let her eyes drop to the floor. "Thank you."

An awkward, yet welcoming and comfortable silence hung in the air.

"Shall we go?" Tradd asked.

Sunlyn nodded, grabbed her matching clutch, and locked the door.

Arriving at the Seafood Carousel in Calabash, they chose to sit outside on the back deck along the waterway. The soft evening breeze pushed most of the humidity from the air. The covered deck had seashell-shaped white lights strung across the top and wrapped around the railings. Sitting outside Sunlyn and Tradd could watch boats docking in front of the restaurant along the pier.

A server appeared with two menus and glasses of ice water. "Can I bring you something different to drink while you take a few minutes to look over the menu?"

"I'd like a glass of white wine," Tradd said. Opening his mouth for a quick second, he closed it and looked at her. "Sorry. What would you like me to order for you?"

Sunlyn smiled. "I'll have the same." The server nodded and went to the bar.

Sunlyn picked up her menu, scanning the dinner options. Closing her eyes for a moment, she let the breeze dance across her face as calmness set in. This wasn't so bad. Sitting outside removed a lot of her nervousness. Sunlyn couldn't remember the last time she'd gone out on an official date.

Running the Beach Bum Beanery didn't allocate much extra time for dating. Not to mention, most of the guys she met were on the island temporarily, either on vacation for a few weeks, or were escaping the snowy months from up north. There were a few men she'd dated off and on, but not much came from it. Sunlyn liked the long hours of commitment the beanery demanded, but the men usually didn't.

Sunlyn felt Tradd's eyes on her, and she slowly matched his gaze, feeling a bit self-conscious. "What?" she asked, setting down the menu. One of her hands touched the top of her head. "You're looking at me like I have horns sticking out or something."

"I'm just thinking."

"About what?"

"This. This is nice. That's all." Tradd cleared his throat. "Do you know what you want?"

"Um," she uttered, looking back at her menu. "Yes. The scallops. You?"

"I think I'll order the shark steak."

The server reappeared and took their orders.

Tradd cleared his throat, listening to the soft jazz music playing in the background. Most tables were full of people enjoying themselves.

"So, tell me," he said. "What do you do for a living?"

"What? You know what I do," Sunlyn stammered.

"Do I, though?" Two dimples emerged on his cheeks as he smiled. "Aren't we supposed to be starting over . . . getting to know each other again?" His brows waggled.

Sunlyn burst into laughter, and just like that, they were 18 again. Laughing and talking with each other as if no time had passed.

The server set their plates in front of them on the table. "If you need anything else, let me know," he said.

Tradd cut a bite of shark. Stabbing it with his fork, he reached across the table toward Sunlyn. "Try this."

Sunlyn's fingers wrapped around Tradd's as she guided the bite into her mouth. Her taste buds awakening from the meaty texture of the pan-seared shark in butter and olive oil, with a twinge of Cajun spice. The feel of his fingers under hers electrified her nerve endings.

Leaning back in her chair, she swiped her tongue across her lips. "Mm, delicious." In turn, she stabbed one of her scallops and dropped it onto Tradd's steak. It was safe that way. She didn't want to risk finger contact again so soon, not if she was going to have the same reaction.

Finishing their dinner, they each ordered another glass of wine. Sunlyn leaned back in her chair, taking a sip. "So, tell me. What do you like best about New York?"

"The craziness of it all."

"Really?"

"Yep. You learn to move full-throttle if you're going to survive in the city that never sleeps."

"I see." Sunlyn swallowed. "What do you like least, then?"

"That you're not there."

Sunlyn gasped.

"I'm sorry." Tradd was quick to correct himself.

"So . . . you like . . . that I'm not there, then?" Sunlyn asked, studying his face.

Tradd had no answer to her catch-22. Consternation settled over his face, and his eyes dropped to his plate.

Sunlyn giggled. "Oh, relax, will you. I'm just teasing." Leaning across the table, she playfully hit his hand. Another charge surged through her.

Tradd blew a sigh of relief, catching her hand in his, lacing their fingers together. "Can I tell you something embarrassing?"

"Well, that depends."

"On what?" His eye twitched.

"For whom is it embarrassing?" she asked.

"Me." Tradd shrugged. "A group of women came into The Gathering Place the evening before I flew here. And . . ."

"—And?" Was her voice wobbly? She needed to get a grip. One instant, Sunlyn was enjoying a familiar, cozy evening with Tradd. In the next beat, her pulse raced with the subtle flirting that had seemed to come so naturally, and so quickly, to their interactions.

"And. Well, I only saw them from the back. One of the women had hair like yours. Long, blonde, beautiful." He swallowed. "I thought . . . I thought . . . it was . . ." His voice trailed off.

"Finish what you were saying," Sunlyn prodded, removing her hand from his and wrapping it around her wine glass.

"I thought she was you." Tradd coughed into his hand. "I thought you came to my restaurant."

Sunlyn cocked her head, not knowing what she should say. Had he been waiting for her to show up there all these years? Out of the blue. Without an invitation. Her thoughts raced toward her saved text messages. Were they both waiting for the other one to make the next move? To be bold. Brave.

"Aren't you going to say something?" Tradd asked, interrupting her musings.

"While we're sharing things, I have an admission of my own."

"What is it?"

Sunlyn swallowed, her cheeks casting a light pink sheen. "Twenty years ago." Were her hands sweating? They felt clammy. "When you first arrived in Canada, and you texted and called me . . . well—"

"—What?"

"I saved them." As the words fell from her lips, the wine glass slipped from Sunlyn's hand, hitting off the plate and shattering into a million shards on top of the table.

The server rushed to their table. "Please, let me clean this up. We don't want you cutting yourself."

Sunlyn stuttered. "I'm sorry, it just slipped out of my hand."

The server smiled. "No worries. It happens."

Tradd stood, motioning for Sunlyn to do the same. "Before you clean our mess, can I have the check? We'll get out of your way."

The server tore their receipt from his pad, handing it to Tradd.

After paying the bill, Tradd cupped Sunlyn's elbow with his hand, leading her toward his car. Neither spoke on the drive home, both content to listen to the radio and process the other's confession.

Twenty minutes later Tradd pulled in front of Sunlyn's beach house. Getting out of the car, he walked Sunlyn to the steps that led up to her home.

"I can take it from here," Sunlyn said.

"So, you saved my messages and texts, huh?"

Sunlyn rubbed her head and softly chuckled.

"How many times did you read them?" he asked in a teasing manner.

"What?"

"You heard me. How many times over the years did you read my texts? Once a week? Once a month? Several times a year?" he teased. "Yesterday? Today? Come on, you can tell me." Tradd stepped closer, letting his hands come to rest on her shoulders.

"You know, Tradd Morrison, you're such a guy!" Sunlyn pursed her lips. "I plead the Fifth."

"Oh no. You're not allowed to. Haven't you read the "confession handbook" of what you can and cannot say?"

"You're crazy, Tradd," Sunlyn said, laughing.

"Come on, tell me," Tradd said, stepping closer.

Tradd's closeness flustered her. Sunlyn took a deep breath. She could smell the scent of freshly laundered clothes. Did he smell like Tide or All? No. Neither. He smelled better than laundry detergent.

Sunlyn jutted her head, chortling. "I cannot confirm how many times I may have or may not have read them."

It was dark. The sun had set long ago. Their only light was from the moon and from the small lights on the banister of her stairs. It was enough, though. Enough for Sunlyn to watch helplessly as Tradd closed the space between them, his mouth searching-out hers. Their lips clung to each other's while her heart raged against her chest.

And then she knew his scent.

He smelled like sunshine.

Was that even a thing?

It didn't matter. At that moment Sunlyn knew she was in trouble.

SEVENTEEN

Sunlyn greeted Mary the next day with a cup of espresso and a plate with two mini lemon muffins.

Sliding her purse on the shelf below the counter, Mary slid her apron over her clothes.

"Okay," she said, tapping her foot on the floor, "what gives?"

"Oh, puh-lease! You act as though you never drink coffee or taste-test the baked goods," Sunlyn stated, strutting across the room to a table. "Come join me."

Skeptical, Mary carried her cup and plate over to where Sunlyn sat. She took a tiny sip of the espresso. "I'm glad you're using this. It's a nice addition to the beanery."

"Right!"

Mary stared at Sunlyn. Something was different. Her friend seemed happier. Lighter. Not the kind of "lighter" from losing weight but the kind of "lighter" from releasing the weight of the world from her shoulders. Bringing the muffin to her mouth, Mary nibbled the lemony goodness.

"Oh my, Sunlyn. This is really good, especially the icing."

"Thanks, Mary."

"Okay . . . out with it," Mary mumbled through another bite. Then, as if something clicked, Mary had a coughing fit. "Last night—" More coughs. "You talked with Tradd!" She drank some coffee to clear her throat.

Sunlyn's eyes sparkled. "Yes, I did."

"So . . . are you going to tell me, or am I expected to drag it out of you?" Mary propped her elbows on the edge of the table, resting her chin in her hands.

"It was nice. We agreed to try again."

Clapping her hands, Mary's eyes lit up. "That's wonderful! You guys are getting a second chance at love."

"Uh-huh. Tradd termed it as getting to know each other again and not just picking up where we left off years ago."

"I'm so happy for you, Sunlyn. Now I don't have to worry as much—"

Sunlyn's head tipped. "—About what?"

"Leaving. I know there'll be someone back here in your corner."

"At least temporarily. There is the issue of living states away."

"But in today's world, you two are just a plane ride away. A couple hours." Mary looked at her friend. She slid her hand across the table and squeezed Sunlyn's hand. "Don't forget that. Keep your heart open."

Sunlyn nodded, squeezing Mary's hand in return.

"Promise me," Mary insisted.

"I promise," Sunlyn said.

Just then, as if on cue, Tradd walked into the beanery. "Good morning, ladies," he greeted as his eyes caught the glimmering espresso machine behind the counter.

Tradd looked at the two of them, pleased that Sunlyn was already using the new coffee machine. The looks on their faces told him that he had walked into the middle of a serious conversation. His timing had always been off when it came to Sunlyn. Seems that it still was, but at least her smile told him she didn't mind.

Behind Tradd a ruckus group of teenagers strolled inside. Mary stood, eyes darting from Tradd to Sunlyn.

"You two talk. I'll handle the teenie-boppers."

Tradd sat where Mary was. "Would you like to help me paint the inside of my mother's house tomorrow?"

"You're starting that project?" Sunlyn asked, finishing the last sip of her espresso.

"I thought if I did, maybe the house would sell faster." Tradd watched Sunlyn take a deep breath and exhale. It was probably still a touchy subject, with her knowing that once he got the house ready to sell, he'd be heading back to New York. But the painting would give them more time together.

"I see. Sure. I'm off tomorrow. What time?"

"Great. Is 8:00 a.m. too early?"

"Early?" Sunlyn giggled, standing. "For a baker, that's heaven. I get to sleep for a few extra hours." She held her index finger up for him to wait at the table. "I'll be right back."

Tradd warmed. This was nice, seeing her every day again. He watched as she walked across the beanery, put something into a bag, and made him an espresso in a to-go cup. Crossing back to the table where they sat, Sunlyn looked happy, happier than when he'd first arrived a couple of weeks ago.

As she got closer, he stood to meet her. Sunlyn extended the bag and cup.

"Here, it's on the house."

"What is it?"

"An espresso from my new machine and mini lemon muffins. I baked early this morning. Let me know what you think later."

"I'd be happy to." Tradd took the items from her hands, his knuckles brushing against her fingers. He loved the feel of her hand against his. *Focus, man!* "I'll see you in the morning, then."

"I'll bring the coffee."

"It's a date—" Tradd blurted. Then he remembered she didn't like that term. "I mean—"

"—No, no." Sunlyn smiled warmly. "It's a date."

Looking from side to side, Tradd leaned in, placing a quick peck on her lips. "Until then."

EIGHTEEN

Sunlyn's eyes darted back and forth as she walked into Tradd's mother's house. Dropcloths were strewn across the furniture and floors haphazardly, and two wooden ladders stood in each room. Each ladder boasted a can of paint and a roller on the little shelf near the top.

Sunlyn set the thermos of coffee on the kitchen island while her eyes roamed over Tradd. He was wearing a pair of worn jeans that had a large hole in one of the knees and tattered hems. His graphic T-shirt had a cracked picture of Spiderman across the front.

"What?" Tradd asked.

Sunlyn rolled her eyes. *Busted.* "Nothing," she lied. It was totally something. She liked this relaxed version of Tradd. "Um, where do you want to start?"

"First things first." Tradd stepped closer, embracing Sunlyn. "Good morning." He kissed the top of her head.

Closing her eyes, just for a second or two, she caught his scent again. He definitely smelled like sunshine. "Good morning," she mumbled in return, knowing she could stay like this forever.

"I'll let you start in here, and I'll start in the living room."

"Do you mind if I put music on while I paint?" she asked.

"Go for it."

"Where did you get all this stuff?" she asked, motioning toward the rooms.

"I found them in the storage shed under the deck. I guess my mom had some work done on the house."

"They're coming in handy, that's for sure." She glanced down at the white drop-cloths covered with different-colored paint splotches.

Sunlyn pulled her phone from the pocket of her old, blue-jean shorts and climbed the ladder.

Reluctantly, Tradd went into the living room and climbed the ladder. He had chosen very light-blue paint for the top half of the walls, then afterward he'd planned on applying white wainscoting to the bottom half of the walls.

Some might think the look was outdated, but not Tradd. He'd always enjoyed the look. It gave the rooms an airy feeling, as it should feel, living on Sunset Beach.

Dipping his roller into the tray of paint, he heard the song "You Make My Dreams," by Hall & Oates, blaring from the other room.

Perched on top of the ladder, Tradd was at the perfect angle to watch Sunlyn painting. He couldn't believe she still listened to that group. It was her favorite duo from their teenage years. He chuckled as she sang along. His thoughts drifted back to the time Tom Bean had let them repaint the coffee shop. She had put on Hall & Oates then, too. And she had looked so cute singing into her paintbrush that Tradd had rushed across the room to give her a kiss—their first.

"—Spiders!" Sunlyn screamed disrupting Tradd's thoughts.

Watching Sunlyn's body jerk on the top rung of the ladder, Tradd yelled. "Sunlyn, stop moving like that!"

"I can't help it!" she hollered. "They're all over the ladder!"

Practically jumping from his ladder, he rushed into the kitchen just in time to see the rickety ladder teeter back and forth. "The ladders are too old!" he yelled again.

The ladder teetered too far to the other side as Sunlyn tried climbing down the rungs. And then it completely upset, tossing Sunlyn to the floor with the tray of paint following, landing on top of her head.

Too late to save her, Tradd skidded to a stop.

Blue paint oozed from the tray, covering her blonde hair and shoulders.

"Oh my," Tradd sputtered, feeling like he had stepped into a scene straight from "I Love Lucy." Squatting in front of her, Tradd bit his lip to keep from laughing. "Are you okay?"

Sunlyn's green eyes looked at him, shell-shocked. Nodding, she mumbled. "I . . . hate . . . spiders."

Tradd burst out laughing. No longer squatting, he sat on the floor near her, his feet and legs twisted like a pretzel.

"It's not funny," Sunlyn whined.

"Yes, it is," Tradd muttered through his laughter.

"Well," Sunlyn squeaked, running one hand through her hair. She looked at her paint-covered hand, then at Tradd. He watched her lip starting to tremble as if she was on the verge of crying. "I guess it's a little funny." Sunlyn laughed. "I hate spiders. There must have been 100 of them on that ladder."

"Really, Sunlyn,100?"

She changed her count. "Okay, maybe 50."

"Seriously?" Tradd asked.

"Fine. There were only two, but that doesn't change the fact that I hate spiders!"

In the next instant, Sunlyn leaned in closer. Her hand landed firmly on top of Spiderman. Leaning back, she laughed.

"Serves Spidey right. He didn't save me," Sunlyn said as matter of fact.

Looking down at his T-shirt with a campy expression, Tradd saw Sunlyn's handprint covering

Spiderman's face. Tradd latched onto Sunlyn's arms, gently pulling her toward him. In the next beat, his mouth claimed hers in a tempestuous kiss. Their mouths clung to each other as his heart thundered in his ears.

A rush of familiarity engulfed Tradd. Yet, this kiss wasn't anything like their first kiss, which was awkward and swift. Of course, getting busted in the middle of it by her uncle didn't help matters.

No. This kiss was different.

It was a toe-curling, pulse-jumping kiss.

The kind of kiss that had Tradd wishing it would last forever.

Putting the brakes on their kiss, his heart clenched as he stood, then helped Sunlyn to stand as well. "You can use the shower in the guest room. There are towels, and you can borrow my robe while I wash your clothes."

"What about your walls? We're a long way from finishing."

"I think we've each had enough for today."

Relieved, Sunlyn smiled. "Better wash your T-shirt too, before the paint dries." Her eyes dropped to his shirt.

"No way," Tradd said. "I'm keeping your handprint. It's right over my heart."

An hour later Sunlyn found Tradd sitting outside on the deck. Stepping onto the deck, she was surprised to feel her heart jump into her throat. Not only did he smell like sunshine, but he also felt like home to her again.

"Come sit," he said, smiling.

Sunlyn crossed the deck and was about to sit on the chair next to Tradd, but he stopped her. "Not there. Here," he said, patting his legs.

She caught her breath.

Then she smiled while obeying, noticing that he had changed his T-shirt. She exhaled while snuggling into him.

Tradd reached, stroking her wet hair tenderly. "I can still see a few strands of blue."

Sunlyn held her breath. His tender touch caused her insides to betray her. Her heart rate skipped a few beats while her stomach fought the butterflies furiously fluttering inside. Trying to calm her insides, Sunlyn found it nearly impossible. Every part of her protested her efforts, yearning for the closeness he offered.

"I guess I'm going to give Mary a run for her money when it comes to streaks of color in our hair." Sunlyn giggled, resting her head on his shoulder.

A welcome silence fell between them.

Caressing her cheek with his thumb, Tradd's eyes pivoted to a lone American Coot flying into the saltmarsh, squawking as it settled into the protective wetland.

NINETEEN

Tradd stepped from his shower the following morning smiling as his eyes saw his graphic tee hanging on the hook in his bathroom. He couldn't have imagined reconnecting with Sunlyn the way he had.

He was happy.

He was in love.

Wait! Did I just think of the "L" word?

Tradd looked at his reflection in the mirror. "You betcha," he spoke out loud. Walking into his bedroom, he threw on a polo shirt and stepped into a pair of shorts and brown loafers. Just then his cell phone rang.

Sitting on the edge of his bed, he grabbed it, and answered.

"Mitch, what's going on?"

"We need you back here."

Tradd's throat tightened. *Not now,* he thought. "What's going on?" Tradd knew that eventually he'd have to head back to New York. Eventually. Not this soon, though. Not when things had been going so well with Sunlyn.

"Three servers quit—"

"—Call the agency and place an ad online." Tradd released the breath he hadn't realized he was holding. Easy fix.

"And Jock," Mitch added.

Now that was a problem. Jock was Tradd's head chef, hired from day one. He was irreplaceable. And it wasn't as if you could just call an agency to fill his place. It took time to find a new chef.

"What happened?"

"He was offered a position at Empire Dining."

"'Empire Dining.' I never heard of it."

"It's some fancy-schmancy place that just opened in the Empire State Building. They made Jock a good offer. Along with the three servers."

This can't be happening. "So . . . counteroffer. I don't want to lose Jock."

"I did," Mitch answered.

Tradd felt like he'd been punched in the gut. He crossed his room to the window, peering outside. Not a bird to be seen.

"Okay. Offer Jock's assistant, Bryce, triple pay . . . temporarily, to pick up the slack." Tradd knew what he had to do. "I'll fly back this evening and take care of things."

"I'm sorry, Boss."

"It's all good. Besides, I've been itching to get back in the kitchen to try new recipes."

"What about Sunlyn?" Mitch asked. "I'm guessing that since you've been MIA, things have been going well?"

The last few weeks passed in front of Tradd's eyes. "Actually, they have."

"How's she gonna take the news?"

"Time will tell. I'll pack, then head over to her coffee shop and break the news."

"Good luck, Tradd—" A loud crash of glass breaking in the background interrupted Mitch. He shook his head. "Mia's at it again. I'd better go. But, hey, do you need me to pick you up at the airport?"

"I'll take a cab. Thanks, anyway. See you later tonight." Tradd swiped the icon, ending their conversation.

As he packed his suitcase, Tradd's thoughts held him captive. He was unsure how Sunlyn would take the news. She was finally letting down that protective wall she'd built. Now she was going to think he was abandoning her. At the same time Mary was. But that couldn't be further from the truth, and deep down, he had to believe she knew that too.

A few hours later Tradd secured and locked the beach house and tossed his suitcase into the trunk of his rental car. He had stalled long enough. Tradd couldn't put off seeing Sunlyn any longer if he was going to make his flight on time.

Pulling in front of the Beach Bum Beanery, he sighed. At least the shop didn't look too busy. Usually, it had a steady stream of customers trickling inside, starting early morning and continuing into the evening. Climbing out of his car, he meandered inside.

Sunlyn was wiping off the counter when she spotted him. Flashing Tradd a grin, she finished wiping the countertop.

"Hi, Tradd."

"Hey." *If she only knew.* "We need to talk." That didn't come out right. Why did he choose those words? Nothing good ever came from "'We need to talk.'" *Way to go!*

He watched as Sunlyn's head cocked and her brows shot up. "Okay," she said, in a low, drawn-out way.

"Let's sit down," Tradd mumbled, motioning toward one of the tables.

"I prefer to stand right where I am," she stated, her voice guarded.

This was going to be more difficult than he'd thought. Her walls had gone right back up. Might as well just blurt it out. Like ripping off a bandage.

"Mitch called this afternoon. My head cook and half my staff quit on the spot and took jobs at a competing restaurant. I'm flying back to New York." There. Bandage gone.

Her face blanched, but her features deadpanned. "When?"

Tradd glanced at his phone, checking the time. "In a few hours."

"You mean, as in today?"

Tradd nodded.

"How long will you be gone?"

"I'm not sure. It takes time to interview and hire a new head chef that jives with the place."

"Oh."

Tradd reached across the counter, touching her hand. "I'm sorry. You know I'll be back. We're just getting started. I'm coming back."

"I mean . . ." She swallowed. "You say that. But how do I know that?" She withdrew her hand from under his.

"You need to trust me. I'm coming back."

"When?" She folded her arms in front of her, jutting her chin at Tradd. "Twenty years?" Her shoulders heaved with a large breath. "I know, I know." She held her hands up in the air to stop him from talking. "It's long distance. This is what happens. Your livelihood is in New York. You live in New York. And." Sunlyn's hands swept through the beanery. "I live here. In Sunset Beach."

"Sunlyn, it's going to work out fine. You'll see."

Tradd hated this. But the facts were the facts; this was long distance. They could make it work. He *would* make it work. He knew for sure this wasn't going to end like it did years ago. He wouldn't let it. They were older now. More mature.

"You keep saying that. But those are empty words. How do I know that you're really coming back?"

"Because, I said I will. We're adults. We're not kids anymore."

Sunlyn shook her head, walking around the counter. She stopped in front of Tradd, looking him straight in the eyes. "Tell me, Tradd."

"I . . ." Tradd's hands were clammy. Looking down at them and then back at Sunlyn, he cleared his throat. "Because . . ." Tradd's throat tightened.

"Because why?" Sunlyn challenged.

"Because . . . I . . ." Tradd stammered, smacking his lips together as if he'd eaten cotton balls. What was so hard about telling her he was in love with her? Three simple little words, and he couldn't spit them out.

He studied her face. Sunlyn looked sad. Hurt. Guarded. Brick by brick, the walls were going higher. All he needed to do was tell Sunlyn what she needed to hear. And he couldn't. Not now. It wasn't the right time when he was on the verge of flying back to New York.

"Say it," she demanded. "Tell me."

Tradd's cheeks flushed. What was wrong with him? His mouth opened, but nothing came out. He stood, watching as Sunlyn crossed her shop and opened the door.

"Go ahead and leave, Tradd. I don't care." Her foot furiously tapped off the floor.

Tradd walked through the open door, stopping outside. "I'll be back. I promise."

Sunlyn shook her head. "Leave, Tradd. New York is waiting!"

Tradd's head lolled as he walked to his car. Climbing inside and starting the vehicle, he looked up to see that Sunlyn had already gone back inside and closed the door behind her.

Tradd sighed and backed out of the parking lot, determined to find the most perfect timing to express his feelings.

TWENTY

Sunlyn's head pounded. Almost closing time. Twice this afternoon since Tradd had dropped his bombshell, Sunlyn had dumped the contents of her purse on the countertop in search of Tylenol. She had a massive headache.

Served her right, she scolded herself. She knew better than to get involved again with Tradd. This was what she got. His life in Manhattan won. Deep down she knew he'd never be happy staying in Sunset Beach.

Sunlyn grunted. *Stupid girl!*

He as much as said that to her when he invited her to move to New York, offering her the position of pastry chef at The Gathering Place. Talk about wearing rose-colored glasses. How could she be so blind to the fact he would never settle into her simple life. She was the one that had to change her life.

For him.
His way.
His life.
His restaurant.
His city.

The way he'd always wanted. Or otherwise, why did he ask her to relocate to New York? He'd never asked her what she wanted. Sunlyn felt stuck between the past and the present. Why couldn't Tradd just admit his feelings to her?

Sunlyn was truly alone now. It was only a matter of a few weeks until Mary moved to the West Coast. First her parents, then Tradd, then her uncle, and finally Mary.

At least she still had the company of the sandpipers.

Blowing out a puff of hot air, Sunlyn couldn't cross the beanery fast enough to lock the door. She flipped the sign to "Closed" and, locking the door, turned to walk back toward the counter. The sooner she swept the floor, the sooner she could go home.

As soon as she grabbed the broom, the door unlocked and Mary burst through, running straight into her.

"Sunlyn!" Mary screamed with tears running down her face. "Sunlyn!"

Sunlyn dropped the broom and grabbed Mary by the shoulders, her heart pounding. "What is it? What's wrong?"

But Mary was laughing.

"Mary, tell me!"

Mary sniffed. "Ry—an—" she muffled between sobs.

"Did something happen to Ryan?"

"No," Mary blubbered, her shoulders heaving as she tried to calm herself. "We're staying here. We're not moving," she hollered.

"Are you serious?" Sunlyn asked, blinking.

"Yes!" Mary grabbed onto Sunlyn's arms. "I mean, Ryan will have to go for about a month to train the new management. But he told his bosses we want to stay, and they're letting us stay in North Carolina."

Sunlyn's eyes grew wide. "So, you're staying? You're not leaving?"

"No, silly! We're staying!" Mary hollered, laughing.

"You're staying!" Sunlyn screamed, eyes stinging with tears of relief. She wasn't going to be alone after all. Still holding onto each other, they jumped up and down, screaming and crying. "Wait until Tradd hears . . ." Sunlyn's voice trailed off the second his name rolled off her lips.

Sunlyn let go of Mary's shoulders, walked back to where she'd dropped the broom, and picked it up again. Her headache had disappeared as soon as Mary entered the room. Now it was back.

Mary followed and touched her shoulder.

"What's the matter, Sunlyn?" Mary asked.

Sunlyn shook her head.

Mary reached for the broom, causing Sunlyn to stop what she was doing. "Look at me. I'm going to ask you one more time. And . . . I don't want to hear the word "'nothing'" coming from your lips. We're supposed to be there for each other. Except—"

"—Except what?" Sunlyn shot back.

"I haven't been. This moving thing had me so wrapped up in my own problems that I've neglected you. Can you forgive me?" Mary pulled Sunlyn into her arms, hugging her.

"There's nothing to forgive." Sunlyn squeezed her back. Hard.

Mary pulled away, brushing Sunlyn's long blonde hair from her face. "Wait a minute," Mary said, her eyes narrowing. "What's in your hair?" She pulled a few strands out to the side, canvassing them. "Did you get blue highlights?" Mary asked in falsetto fashion.

Sunlyn burst with laughter, perching on top of the counter. Her favorite seat in the place when the Beach Bum Beanery closed. She could still hear her uncle telling her to get down, that it looked bad to the customers, even with no customers in the shop.

"No." Sunlyn shook her head. Mary always knew how to cheer her up by saying just the right thing at the right time. "That's paint from when I helped Tradd paint his mother's house."

Mary scratched her chin. "But weren't you supposed to paint the walls, not give yourself highlights?" she asked, waggling her eyebrows.

"It's a long story that involves spiders, rickety ladders, and a paint tray falling on my head."

Mary giggled. "That can't be what's got you so down, especially with me running around with purple streaks in my hair."

"Tradd's gone," Sunlyn barely whispered.

"What?"

"Tradd left. He's gone," Sunlyn said a bit louder. "Do you have Tylenol?"

"Sorry, no Tylenol. Why did he leave?"

"I don't know, something about his cook and servers quitting, leaving him in the lurch."

Mary stepped closer and playfully hit her friend's knee. "I can see that. Can't you? It's his restaurant. He'll be back, won't he?"

Sunlyn gave Mary a quizzical look. "I guess."

"You guess?"

"Well, I mean, Tradd—"

"—But?" Mary cut in.

"I don't believe him."

"Why not?"

"Because it's like we rewound time to twenty years ago. He couldn't say it then, and he can't say it now."

"What isn't he saying?"

"That he loves me," Sunlyn blurted, jumping from her perch. "Why would he come back to me if he can't even bother to tell me what I need to hear?"

"Does he know this?"

"Yes. We've talked about it. That's the thing that changed our course twenty years ago. And he's doing it again. Today." Sunlyn ran her fingers through her long strands. "I can't do this again. I can't wait twenty years for him to show up and expect us to pick up where we left off. I won't do it!"

"Wow."

"I know, right." Sunlyn folded her arms in front of her, biting her lip. Biting back the tears that threatened to spill.

"No. I mean wow . . . you."

"Excuse me?"

Mary pushed Sunlyn toward a table. "Sit." Then Mary knelt in front of her friend, looking her straight in the eyes.

"Look, I know you've been hurt, and you have that stupid wall protecting your heart, but enough is enough. Girlfriend, you need to swallow that pride of yours and tell him first."

Sunlyn's face paled. "You want me to tell him that I love him first! Are you serious?"

"Someone has to say it. Why not you?" Mary leaned back on her heels, studying Sunlyn's face. "What year is this? And don't answer that, it's rhetorical. There are a lot of lonely people walking around in this world because they're too afraid to say something."

"But he's in . . . New York."

"Who cares. In today's world that's a blink of an eye. Go to him, Sunlyn. Tell him."

Sunlyn jumped from her chair, brushing past Mary. "I can't fly to New York. What about my coffee shop?"

"I'm here. Remember me?" Mary stood. "Stop making excuses. If you love him, you'll be on the next plane out of here."

Sunlyn looked at Mary. "But . . ."

Mary crossed her arms.

"But . . ." Sunlyn uttered. "I don't have an overnight bag."

"Use one of mine. Heck, use a plastic bag, I don't care. Just tell him!"

TWENTY-ONE

Seated on the plane and gripping the armrest of her window seat, Sunlyn fixed her gaze on the tiny white lights below as the plane flew higher into the night sky, until she could no longer see anything but vast darkness.

Why did she let Mary talk her into this craziness? Not only did Mary schedule her redeye flight, but she also booked her a room at the airport Marriott. Then Sunlyn could sleep before spending the next day exploring Manhattan and then stopping in to see Tradd.

Still unsure she should be following Tradd to the Big Apple, she decided she could always plead temporary insanity and grab the next flight back to Myrtle Beach as soon as she landed in New York.

New York. Sunlyn sighed, resting her head against the back of the seat. She was really doing this.

Sunlyn couldn't wait to see Tradd.
To tell him.
And to hear her words reciprocated.

Sunlyn climbed from the cab and onto the sidewalk across the street from The Gathering Place. She swallowed as warmth traveled through her. It was now or never.

Sunlyn had spent most of the day visiting Central Park, the Empire State Building, St. Patrick's Cathedral, and even Tiffany's, a store she had always wanted to visit. Even though she'd known that she would come back from the shopping excursion empty-handed.

The sidewalks in Manhattan were still congested at 9:30 in the evening. People rushed everywhere, walking with purpose. No one dawdled. Sunlyn had heard New York was the city that never slept. Now she believed it.

The Gathering Place looked busy. A crowd of people was waiting outside on the sidewalk to get in. Crossing the busy street, she took her place at the back of the small crowd. Surprisingly, it moved swiftly, and then it was her turn.

Sunlyn stepped inside Tradd's dream.

The restaurant was alive, buzzing with people talking and laughing. Tables were dressed in gold-colored linens with crystal water-goblets. The chandeliers hanging from the ceiling cast a soft glow onto the patrons. Servers rushed from table to table, tending to everyone's needs.

A large bar stood to the left of the room, where people gathered for a drink while waiting for their dining reservations. The wall behind the bar was a mirror that reflected light onto the bottles of alcohol, making the liquid inside sparkle and shine.

Her heart fluttered, knowing Tradd had accomplished his dream. His vision. And it was absolutely beautiful. She was proud of him. Of course he needed to return to The Gathering Place to handle the sudden staff changes.

Her eyes darted from the servers to the hostess in hopes of catching a glimpse of Tradd. His restaurant was busy. There were a lot of people to sift through. Then she spotted him. He was closer than she'd realized.

Tradd was standing behind the bar talking to a woman. The woman he was speaking with was gorgeous. Brunette. Tall. And had red painted lips.

Sunlyn took a few steps toward them. In the next beat, the woman jumped with excitement, throwing her arms around Tradd's neck and kissing him on the cheek.

Sunlyn stopped in her tracks, and glasses on a server's tray clattered together as he swerved to miss her.

Tradd looked up. At her.

In a matter of seconds every imaginable thought Sunlyn could think of bounced through her mind. And as if in slow motion, she watched as Tradd removed the woman's arms from his neck and started toward her.

No! Sunlyn forced her feet to move. Turning, she ran out of the restaurant. She would not let him fill her head with lies about what he was doing with the brunette.

No wonder he was in such a hurry to return to New York. And no wonder he didn't know when he'd return to Sunset Beach. And most of all, no wonder he wouldn't tell her that he loved her.

Her vision blurred from tears as she reached the sidewalk. Weaving between the people on the sidewalk, she heard her name. Sunlyn continued running, refusing to look back. Reaching the street corner, she noticed a couple getting out of a taxi. She dove into the backseat, instructing the driver to take her back to the airport.

Skidding to a stop on the sidewalk just outside his restaurant, Tradd watched helplessly as Sunlyn slipped through the crowd and into a cab. He'd much rather chase after her in another taxi, just like a scene out of a movie, but he had responsibilities to tend to at The Gathering Place.

Whipping around on the sidewalk, Tradd headed back inside. What had just happened? He didn't know Sunlyn was coming. Why hadn't she told him? He could have picked her up at the airport. Scheduled time with her. Shared his heart with her and let her know what he was planning.

Shaking his head, he weaved through the servers, heading back toward his office. Once inside, he sat in his chair, looking at the stack of papers on his desk. Grabbing his cell phone, Tradd called Sunlyn. Several times. All calls went unanswered. In a brief spout of anger and disappointment, his hand swooshed across the top, sending the papers into the air. Lacing his fingers behind his head, Tradd watched as the papers landed on the floor in a heap.

"Whoa, Boss. What's going on?" Mitch asked, standing in the doorway.

Tradd heaved his shoulders, blowing out a puff of hot air, and raked his fingers through his dark hair. "Sunlyn was here."

"At the restaurant?" Mitch asked.

Tradd nodded. "Yep." Slipping from his chair he bent, proceeding to pick up the scattered papers. After he and Mitch put them back on the desk Tradd started sorting them, feeling defeated. "I didn't know she was coming. Otherwise, I would've . . ."

"Well . . . where is she now?"

"Who knows. She ran out of here."

"Why?"

"She saw me talking with Mia. I was offering her the job of head bartender, and well, you know Mia. She planted one on my cheek." Tradd leaned back in his chair.

"Didn't you explain to Sunlyn?"

"Never had the chance. Now she thinks I'm two-timing her."

Mitch's brows raised. "That's a tough one," he said, half laughing. "If Sunlyn only knew that Mia and I were dating . . ."

"If only," Tradd mumbled. "I need to sort these papers. How's the training going with Mia?"

"Great. She's ready to take over the reins as head bartender, and then I can step into my new position."

"Good." Tradd looked at Mitch and half-smiled. "Thanks for being here. Don't forget we have two interviews in the morning for head chef."

"Don't you worry, I'll be here."

"Hey, if you don't mind, I'm gonna hide out in my office the rest of the evening. Can you handle the floor?"

Mitch didn't hesitate. "Of course."

"Appreciate that. On your way out, close the door. I have some things I need to figure out."

Mitch pointed his index finger and thumb at his boss, making a clicking sound with his tongue against his cheek and left.

Tradd cradled his head in his hands. As if things weren't confusing enough between him and Sunlyn, Tradd now needed to clear up this debacle. He had to find a way to convey his feelings to Sunlyn.

As he focused on the papers, an idea came to him. Grabbing his cell phone, he searched for the Beach Bum Beanery's number. It was too late. The beanery had already closed for the evening. He would have to wait until tomorrow. Then Tradd could talk with Mary and enlist her help.

TWENTY-TWO

After receiving Tradd's call the following morning, Mary agreed to help. On some level, she blamed herself for what had happened in New York. After all, she had talked Sunlyn into going. All she could do now, was wait for Sunlyn.

Sunlyn strolled into the beanery mid-morning looking as if she had been up all night. Her hair was pulled into a scruffy-looking ponytail, and her eyes were sunken.

"Coffee. I need coffee," Sunlyn uttered, setting her cell phone on the counter.

"What happened to you?" Mary asked. She couldn't remember the last time she'd seen Sunlyn looking this ragged. Mary hurriedly poured Sunlyn a large mug of coffee, handing it to her.

"That's what happened." Sunlyn pointed toward her phone. "I had to finally shut it off. Tradd wouldn't stop calling."

"You didn't answer his calls?" Mary questioned her friend.

"Nope." Sunlyn shook her head defiantly. "I ignored every single one of them."

Mary's head tilted. "You mean you ghosted him. Again. Just like you did twenty years ago?"

Sunlyn's head jerked.

Her mouth opened as if she was going to say something. But nothing came out. A stunned shadow appeared across her face.

"Look, I know I sound rough. You're my best friend in the world. I had to say it. You can't do this to Tradd again. Don't you think you should have taken his calls to see what he had to say?"

"Me!" Sunlyn's temper flared. Stepping back, she set her mug on the counter. "You can't blame this on me. I got my answer in the form of a lanky brunette hanging all over him—kissing him—right in the middle of his restaurant, for everyone to see."

"Seriously, Sunlyn?"

"I saw it," Sunlyn scoffed. "You didn't!"

Mary snorted. It was time to lay her last card on the counter. "And I spoke with him. You didn't!"

Mary watched Sunlyn's brows knit together as she processed what Mary had just said.

"You what?"

"You heard me." Mary leaned against the counter.

"When?"

"This morning. He told me everything." Mary's lips pursed.

"But . . . I don't understand." Sunlyn's temperament softened.

"You will. I need you to do something for me."

"What?"

"You need to leave. Go to the Kindred Spirit Mailbox. Read the journal entries from a few days ago."

"But why?"

"Trust me."

The door to the coffee shop opened. Four people strolled in, straight to the counter.

"I . . . I . . . can't." Sunlyn's eyes flashed toward the customers. "I need to tend to the customers."

Mary reached for Sunlyn's arm and gently squeezed. "I'll take care of them. You need to go to the Kindred Spirit. Now."

Trodding through the uneven sand, Sunlyn hiked to the mailbox.

She loved the feel of the soft sand against her bare feet. This was home. The place she belonged. After witnessing New York, she knew that wasn't the place for her. She could never be happy exchanging sand for concrete.

Admiring the bright-blue sky, she watched as three sea gulls flew without a care in the world. And two black skimmers after that. The small island of Sunset Beach was where she was most comfortable.

Reaching her intended destination and opening the mailbox, Sunlyn's hands began shaking as she pulled out the journal. What was so important on these pages that Mary insisted she read? She felt unnerved.

Sitting on the bench, she opened the journal skimming the recent entries. After a couple minutes, Sunlyn's breath caught in her throat. She held the book closer to her face, devouring the fifteen-word entry scrawled across the page.

Finally, I figured out what took a long, long time. I love you, Sunlyn.

Tradd

Gasping, Sunlyn stared at the page. It was dated the same day he'd left for New York. The words soon became unreadable from tears. Pressing the journal to her chest with her heart clenching, she let them flow freely. She didn't care who saw. Those fifteen words had crumbled her defenses.

TWENTY-THREE

Two days later Tradd Morrison walked into the Beach Bum Beanery, smiling ear to ear. He was back on the island. Right where he belonged—at least, most of the time.

His heart sank as his eyes canvassed the inside of the coffee shop. No Sunlyn.

Tradd strode across the shop toward Mary. She was behind the counter, filling an order. After completing the customer's order, Mary stretched across the counter, arms spread wide. Tradd leaned in, hugging her.

"Welcome back, Tradd!" Mary patted his back.

"Thanks, it's good to be back. Where's—"

"—I believe you'll find her heading to the beach. She said something about taking the pathway at the end of 40th Street. Mumbling something about the seashell tree." Mary shrugged.

"Great!" Tradd took off after Sunlyn. He hadn't mentioned that he was returning, wanting to surprise her.

Fortieth Street ended at a saltmarsh with only four parking spaces. Tradd was lucky enough to snag the last open spot. Stepping from his car, Tradd ran his fingers through his hair. Was he nervous? He must be. He hadn't even taken the time to change out of his business clothes and into casual beachwear. His suitcase sat unopened in the trunk of his rental car. He didn't care. The only thing Tradd cared about was finding Sunlyn.

As he walked on the wooden boardwalk, his dress shoes clicked off the wooden planks. Or was that his heart he heard thundering in his chest? It was humid, and the closer he got to Sunlyn the more the air smelled of saltwater.

He spotted her, right where Mary said she would be. Pausing for a moment, he drank her in. She was beautiful, her blonde hair blowing in the ocean breeze. He quietly laughed to himself, watching as she tried to tame it while, at the same time, trying to hang something on the tree.

He inched closer, hoping his shoes didn't give him away.

"Allow me," he said, grabbing onto her hair and pulling it away from her face.

Sunlyn whipped around, squealed with joy, and threw herself into Tradd's arms. "You're back! I've missed you so much!"

Tradd closed his eyes and squeezed her tightly, not wanting to let her go. "I missed you too."

After a minute or two, Tradd released her. "What are you hanging on the tree?"

"A sand dollar with our initials on it. Now, we'll always be a part of this place." Sunlyn motioned toward the tree with hundreds of shells hanging from it, all with something written on them to preserve visitors' time on the barrier island.

"We need to talk," they said at the same time, laughing.

"Allow me to go first," Tradd said, sidestepping the people trying to pass them on the narrow walkway. He leaned against the railing. "Sunlyn, the woman you saw me with the other night at my restaurant is Mia. There is nothing between us. I had just offered her the position as head bartender. Mia gets—how should I say it? Excitable. She and Mitch are the ones dating. Not me."

"Who is Mitch?"

"He is my head bartender. No, that's not true. He *was* my head bartender. He's now the manager of The Gathering Place. I've worked with Mitch for years. He's the only one I trust to run the restaurant when I'm not there."

"Oh," Sunlyn uttered, embarrassed. She looked at her feet. "I'm sorry, Tradd. I assumed that since you left, she was the reason. And when you couldn't tell me that you love me, I thought that . . . she was the reason." Shrugging, Sunlyn dared a sideways glance at him.

"Did Mary tell you about the Kindred Spirit journal?"

Sunlyn's face lit up brighter than the sun. "Yes!" She jumped up, throwing her arms around Tradd's neck, kissing him. But she didn't kiss him on his cheek. Her lips landed smack in the center of his.

Pulling back from her embrace, Tradd searched her eyes. "And?"

"I saw it, Tradd. I read what you wrote."

"And?" Tradd asked.

"And I love you too!"

"Good, because you know what?"

"No, what?" Sunlyn let her arms drop to her side, waiting for Tradd to answer.

"Because I plan on spending a lot more time here on the island. With you."

"What about The Gathering Place?"

"Mitch can handle things in New York. I'll work as much as I can remotely, going back about once a month for a day or two. Who knows, maybe I'll even scout locations on the mainland and open a second restaurant."

"That's wonderful!"

"It is. But I don't want to talk about The Gathering Place or the Beach Bum Beanery."

"What do you want to talk about, then?"

"This," Tradd said, with such tenderness that Sunlyn gasped. He knelt onto the sand-covered walkway and pulled a small, velvet box from his pocket. Opening it, he turned it around, revealing the marquise diamond ring to Sunlyn.

"Sunlyn, I've known you since the day we crashed into each other with our bikes. We've been best friends, boyfriend and girlfriend, and even strangers." Tradd chuckled. "But we've never been engaged. So, my love, will you marry me and spend all the time in the world that we have as husband and wife?"

Sunlyn had already jutted her hand toward Tradd before he'd finished asking. "Yes, a thousand times, yes! I'll marry you, Tradd Morrison!"

Tradd stood, removing the gold ring from its haven. He slid it onto Sunlyn's finger that was prancing up and down with excitement. His voice hitched. "I love you, Sunlyn Bean."

THREE MONTHS LATER

Deciding their wedding was twenty years in the making, they chose to marry quickly.

Standing on the wet, packed, flat sand, with the ocean tide caressing their bare feet, Sunlyn and Tradd exchanged vows on November 4. Only they, the officiator, and Sunlyn's sandpipers were present. Mary and Ryan stayed at the beanery to prepare a small reception.

Tradd and Sunlyn had picked a spot close to the Kindred Spirit Mailbox. Each dressed in beach clothing, with Sunlyn wearing a white lace, tea-length sundress, and Tradd wearing white linen trousers with rolled cuffs and a button-down shirt.

Sunlyn held a simple, four-piece, pink-carnation bouquet. Each stem a remembrance for her father, mother, uncle, and Tradd's mother. After the ceremony she smiled and tossed the flowers into the tumbling waves.

And just like that, like the ocean tide rolling in and out, the ebb and flow of life continued. The sunset promises that Sunlyn and Tradd had made twenty years ago finally came true.

AUTHOR'S NOTE

The premise for this book was inspired after my husband and I visited Sunset Beach, North Carolina. And yes, I fell in love with the island and the surrounding area and look forward to visiting again in the future.

I highly recommend staying at Sunset Inn, located on Sunset Beach. Area attractions, both on and off the island, are just minutes away from the inn. Tucked along the marsh, the bed & breakfast is only a five-minute walk to the beach. Each room boasts a private, screened porch with rockers, where you can relax in the evening to watch the brilliant sunset, serenaded by some of the island's birds as they settle in for the night.

To find more information about this spectacular inn, hop over to its website. And while you're exploring, don't forget to make your reservation!

www.thesunsetinn.net

I also recommend that you walk along the beach and visit the Kindred Spirit Mailbox. Spend some time reading through the journal entries, and write one of your own. You'll be glad you did. Until you make your own journey to the island, you can learn more about the Kindred Spirit on this website:
www.kindredspiritbox.com

Thank you for taking the time to read

Sunset Promises.

If you enjoyed my story, please leave a positive review.

Reviews are important to authors as they help other readers find new books.

Don't forget to sign up for my newsletter to receive your free book.

It's Only Make-Believe (storyoriginapp.com)

You can learn more about my books at:

susanmellon.com

ABOUT THE AUTHOR

With several books in her catalog, Susan Mellon writes short & sweet romance, specializing in happily-ever-after novellas, that will have you turning the pages.

Susan and her husband, Alex, live in Pittsburgh, Pennsylvania. When not writing, she enjoys reading, watching movies, traveling, live theater, and Pirates baseball. She believes life is too short to eat anything other than premium chocolate and enjoys a glass of raspberry champagne from time to time.